THE PROBLEM WITH UNCLE TEDDY'S MEMOIR

A SPECULATIVE FICTION ROMANTIC ADVENTURE MYSTERY

ED CHARLTON

The Problem with Uncle Teddy's Memoir

ISBNs

Paperback	978-1-935751-24-3
Ereader(Reflowable)	978-1-935751-25-0
Ereader(Fixed Format)	978-1-935751-26-7
Hardback	978-1-935751-27-4

Published in the U.S.A. using American spelling and punctuation despite the work's English setting.

Scribbulations LLC

Kennett Square

Pennsylvania

USA

This book is dedicated to
Grace, of course;
to any family historians who discover the worst;
and to
Akaash and all the future writers.

Thanks to members of The Write Group, Montclair, New Jersey,
and my early readers.

Thanks to Lisa Romeo, Michaela Spampinato, David Henry Sterry,
and Amy Edelman.

THE PROBLEM WITH UNCLE TEDDY'S MEMOIR

The Village Pub
Small Community Publishing

London,

21 May 2011

Hi Theo,

Great to see you last night! Just like old times, must do it again.
These manuscript pages—did you say these were from the rich uncle, or was it the insane one?
I'll have one of my folks read through them, then let's get together for lunch.

Curt

P.S. Please send email address.

T. Kingman

____

____

TheoK@__________.com

24 May 2011

Dear Curt,

Lunch sounds good.

I have more of the manuscript in Aunt Marjory's trunk. I'm working my way through what seem to be two different books, one about architecture, one the memoir. Perhaps we can work up a coherent book from them. I hope the pages I gave you whet your appetite for more.

Please don't let anyone else see the manuscript. It's a bit personal, so I'm not comfortable with anyone but <u>you</u> working on it. The family don't know I have it and I'm a little apprehensive about their reaction when they find out – let's just keep it just between us for now.

It's from Uncle Teddy (Smith), and he wasn't the rich one.

Thanks,

Theo

From the Desk of
Curtis Bookman

Nancy,
Take a look through this for me.
I'll handle all the correspondence.

Curt

in the imperial style; never understated, never in doubt.

If you follow the main Manam Way from the gardens at Pricora northwest almost to its end at The Stone, as you pass the Revelsar warehouses, suddenly below you is the Manam Paravel. None would guess this small park holds a secret. The area is unprepossessing, almost unseen, one of Fate's sleights of hand. It is triangular–precisely triangular–with the hypotenuse lain along the bank of the Manam Way. There is a small fountain at the southern angle and an outcrop of rough stone against the western perimeter that rises to its height at the wider angle.

In that right angle is the singular point of note. There is–what shall I call it?–a cave. Is that to give the feature too much dignity? Does that convey anything of its meaning? But, yes, for now let us call it "a cave."

The grass lawn, short and clean, ends against a flower bed rotated with seasonal blooms and fragrant herbs or rested with mulch. The two paths that meet here join in a dusty scuffing of feet. The children of the Revelsar houses play Hide-and-Seek, Chase-and-Conquer, or Trick-the-Mouse from dawn until dusk. In and out of the cave they run, shouting, calling, whistling, and crying. The stones echo and the sounds carry through the park and up even over the marble balustrade and across the cropped grass of the Manam Way.

The cave is dark, but not deep. Its walls twist to the left and to the right before the roof and floor conspire to block all but the most determined of wrigglers. Beyond the blockage is a chamber–a secret den of fear and delight for small boys and girls. The room holds mementos of courage brought in and left as a dare; dark pebbles wait to be taken back as proof of a challenge faced and accomplished.

Yes, I was there. I was there, small and timid, still young enough to squeeze through to the hidden chamber. I left there a ring, given to me by a distant relative of no great affection. It lies there still, if the protocols of such traditions remain unchanged.

The Manam Paravel, the wedge of green grass, the rocks and seductive cave live in my mind from those early years.

Architecture? page 5

The bright sun, the warm breeze, and the mixed scent of grass and sand were suddenly lost in the cool air of the rock mouth. Once out of the sun, all was dark. Sight slowly adjusted, but until then, all was smell and sound. The scent of damp ground, where the morning's dew had wet the dirt and not been warmed enough to fade, mixed with the smell of bodies hot from running. The sound of breathing magnified and turned until all came back like the voice of a stirring dragon.

A holy place, it seemed. A place of transcendence.

We moved in, hands smoothing the stone as countless others had before. Then, faced with the final obstacle, I lay face down and slid inch by inch through the narrow gap between ceiling and floor, wall and wall, into the true darkness of the hidden chamber. No light entered with me. The others holding vigil so close, not even a faint glimmer could seep in.

Creeping hand-by-finger-by-hand over treasures left and stones yet to be taken, I explored the room, left my token, found a large pebble to claim as mine, and then...?

Then came the true challenge: to find the entrance once more without the aid of my comrades, who stood shoulder to shoulder outside, listening in that tensest of silences.

Nothing has frightened me since.

Nothing can.

From: Bookman@____________.co.uk

Subject: MSS pages

Date: Mon, 06 Jun 2011

To: TheoK@_________.com

Hi Theo,

Reading through the sample, I have a suspicion I've been there. Where is Uncle Teddy writing about? It reminds me of that park by the A5 we used to go to when we bunked out of class. But what's with the foreign-sounding names?

I just did a Google search for your uncle. Why can't I find anything?

Curt

Email TK 06Jun2011

From: Theo < TheoK@_________.com >

Subject: Re: MSS pages

Date: Mon, 06 Jun 2011

To: Bookman@_____________.co.uk

Hi Curt,

Yeah, there are a couple of little problems with Uncle Teddy and his memoir.

I can't really say where the place is yet. Expect more info from the other pages and mementos in Marjory's trunk.

As for Google, I suspect certain family members have been trying whatever they can to make it seem Teddy didn't exist.

Theo

From the Desk of
Curtis Bookman

Nancy,

Have Ellie check into where this might be taking place.
I think I recognize it, but I'm not sure.

Thanks,
Curt

From the Desk of
Nancy Worth

Re: Kingman memoir

Curt,

Ellie found something. Not sure it's what you wanted.

N.

From the Desk of
Ellie Ducet

RE: KINGMAN MEMOIR

NANCY,

DREW A BLANK WITH THE PLACE NAMES. SORRY.

THERE'S A PARK IN EDGWARE THAT FITS THE BILL. IT'S AN EX-QUARRY, BUT IT'S UP AGAINST THE A5 AND IS THE RIGHT SHAPE.

MCCLELLAN PARK:

REDEVELOPMENT AS A PARK, 1935.

ARCHAEOLOGICAL DIG, 1949, FOUND SOME ROMAN ARTIFACTS ASSOC. WITH

OVER

WATLING STREET/ROMAN ROAD.

RE-ZONED 1975 TO BE INCLUDED IN REDEVELOPMENT OF WAREHOUSES (WHICH DIDN'T HAPPEN.)

LET ME KNOW IF YOU NEED ME TO GO DEEPER OR FIND OTHER CANDIDATES.

ELLIE

Email CB 09Jun2011

From: Bookman@____________.co.uk

Subject: Uncle Teddy

Date: Thu, 09 Jun 2011

To: TheoK@________.com

Hi Theo,

Two questions:

When do you think you'll have the completed manuscript?

Is this fiction?

Talk to me.

Curt

From: Theo < TheoK@__________.com >

Subject: Re: Uncle Teddy

Date: Fri, 10 Jun 2011

To: Bookman@______________.co.uk

Hi Curt,

Both good questions. Don't panic. Trust me, this will be worth it.

Uncle Teddy was married to my father's Aunt Marjory. So does that make him a great uncle? I can never work this stuff out.

My grandfather had two siblings, Marjory and Peter. Peter's wife Astelle is still living, though truly ancient. My grandparents, Marjory, Peter, and Teddy himself are all gone. Astelle never approved of Teddy and fell out with Grandfather about it, which I think is why my branch of the family only got a sliver of the family fortune :-(

The family story is that Marjory was Teddy's therapist after he had some kind of accident and lost his memory and, apparently, his use of English. He was very bright and remade himself from scratch. I think you can see, from the pages I gave you, his English became pretty good.

He writes a lot about a city, things that may be reconstructed memories from before his accident. Perhaps that accounts for some of the difficulty.

My father liked Teddy and told me "he had a noble heart." I don't want to see Astelle succeeding in her damnatio memoriae.

Bear with me—I'll get you more of the manuscript as soon as I can type it up. Here is Chapter One to start with.

Must warn you though, the later parts get a bit wild ;-)

Theo

Chapter One

I write at a distance, of course. How far? How far?

In my mind, it is but a step and I see again the fabled towers of Aleronde, the sweep of the skyline, the long straight avenues, the glittering canals, the perfumed air-all but a glance away of the mind's eye.

My home, my youth, my love are Aleronde. Aleronde The Great! Aleronde The Feared! Aleronde The Magnificent! Aleronde The Seat of Wisdom. If I dream of that place when I sleep, it is not a fault of mine, but of where I wake. None can compare. All are lesser. All are dull, drear, darkened copies of that most fine of things. I once thought, *Give me Aleronde or nothing!*

Then I learned better ways. In this book, I shall show both: the golden dream-place of my beginning and the practical, earthy place of my ending.

Marjory is my wife, my nurse, my teacher, my savior, my healer; yet still, she knows little of my past. This shall be for her. Now she will know. If others care to read, perhaps they will understand, perhaps not. It is not for them that I write, but for Marjory, whom I owe a debt unrepayable.

My first memory of Aleronde is of the balcony overlooking Minias Square. I had left a toy in the sun. When I lifted it, a *Srit-la* lay in hiding, trying to shade itself. It frightened me so much Mother came and swept me up in her arms, but the toy flew out of my fingers and over the balcony. Oh, is there ever so tragic a loss as when a precious toy is gone? The world is made of such few treasures at that age and parting with one is so new and raw an experience. Of course, there are worse things in life. Happily, as children we are, for a while, sheltered from that terrible truth.

Of that house, I remember little. It looked over Minias Square at one side, at the other the West Outer Canal. The smell of the spice barges would wake me, and bells round the necks of *Gre-tra* would sing me to sleep.

The house must have had a garden, a roof-walk, a separated worker-house. It may even have had an observatory. I know not. I remember my mother saying that I was the last of her sons to be born there.

***

My younger brother and all my sisters were born in the house I do remember, and I remember their noise above all!

The river Brent, curving wide and slow, bound the garden from the north to the southwest. The house of my youth faced the setting sun. From the doors to the gates was a gentle green slope, carved with tracks of pink stone. Twilight saw the grass turn black and the stones radiate the warmest afterglow.

Before we turn our backs on the night and go in through those doors, I will tell you two memories.

In the long minutes of a fiery sunset, my father stood with his hand on my young shoulder. He told me his plans. He told me his expectations of me. My life lay before me: military service, then private business if I showed aptitude, or public office should that suit me better. His palm was hot through my shirt, though his voice betrayed nothing. I already understood somewhat how much the success of his sons meant to him.

On another night, woken by oncoming sirens, we stood shoulder to shoulder on the veranda. The police chased and killed a rogue Gre-tra before us on the lawn.

As I sit writing this, I hang my head. It is obvious to me now, what I could never have realized then. Then, I saw the shots fired, the twisting of the body, heard the mewling screams, the barked orders. I felt nothing, except perhaps a vague pride—the pride of a son of a pillar of society, the great society of Aleronde. My father watched too, without reaction. I watched without compassion; what was only one Gre-tra amongst so many? And so, now, I sit discomfited. I write at a distance, of course, in a way not far enough.

The entrance hall of the house was a public space, kept forever clean and polished. Nothing was ever out of place, nothing amiss. My mother and her Mut-pel (I recall three who held that position) ensured that father's expectations in this regard were met. Only once or twice did the games of us younger children spill into the hall; games soon ended.

A gift grew there. My father came home one evening and had a mysterious parcel unloaded. Inside was a plant of exquisite delicacy, which would become a monster of thirty feet or more, rising in the indirect sunlight almost to the ceiling within the angles of the staircase. Its long leaves were purple on the underside, while above they shone pale green laced with silver veins. The trunk and branches were white, whiter than any native tree. The gift was from a diplomat, Father said, an emissary on his first visit to Aleronde.

I loved it and, when I could, sat high on the stairs and imagined myself held in the canopy of a forest of such trees, smelling the strange air, listening to the calls of birds I had never seen. There! There it is! My desire to see foreign lands. That romance with the idea of travel. The tree and its imagined birds, swaying in exotic winds! My downfall in the making, my resurrection in miniature.

My father's offices and his library occupied the corridor leading to the right from the hall. Mother had the rooms to the left of the hall for entertaining. The double doors below the balcony led to the dining room. We slept in rooms upstairs and to the left, so that no noise should disturb Father in his offices.

My sisters were the source of most noise. Each could both giggle and scream at the same time; a feat I often marveled at. I was in trouble for noise only when I fought with them or my brothers. Tempers flared over slights and insults, games too well-played, disagreements about things overheard, agreements that one-or-other of us "had it coming." The house did not lend itself to isolation, despite its size. Ours was a family constant in its interactions, unending in its activities, coarse in language, and as quick to react with a blow as with a word. We were fierce children and full of life—like our contemporaries, like our city, like our world.

***

As an adolescent I began to explore the city. Was this partly to escape the family? Perhaps. But living in Aleronde The Great, who could fail to wander? There is so much to be seen; around each corner looms something wonderful, or something old opens to your left or right, while behind you, unnoticed, an architectural splendor waits only for your return.

At the age of sixteen I had passed my first major examination and was permitted an entire day free. I began my explorations with the nearest of The Great Parks. My friends and I called the park "Rugotpaw," a rude twisting of its historical name Roogat Pow, The Remembrance of a Just War.

The centerpiece of the park is the arch. It is one hundred and ten feet high, the number of days the war lasted, and stands astride a circle of thirty-nine segments, the number of battalions deployed.

On its outer sides, the arch has images of the defeated carved into the marble. Inside are the conquering generals, in profile, their names traced out with blue jewels.

The remarkable features of the arch are the adornments at the top. Seven leaping beasts writhe together in crashing waves. The sculpture was controversial, it seems, at the arch's unveiling. The images were too large, too wild, too dynamic. The artists were geniuses, so much is clear—though perhaps their intentions less so.

In my circle of friends, the arguments were at a different level. Firstly, we boys were convinced the monsters were engaged in some freakish orgy. We spent much time speculating on the apparent and hidden aspects of the creatures' anatomy. Secondly, no adult I knew believed such beasts existed. And yet...and yet... The sculpture was permitted, sanctioned, paid for, and placed on permanent display. Aleronde The Mysterious!

Throughout the park, the theme of water and creatures of the sea is repeated and echoed. In the ironwork of the gates, in the fence posts and the lampposts are waves or fish with long snouts and teeth bared. The images on the outer walls of the arch—the faces of the defeated—are not reflected anywhere else. It is as if they were but an afterthought in the celebration of a victorious foreign war.

The path south from Roogat Pow is a narrow walk along a stream, directed in its course by low blue-stone walls, to the next of the historical parks. This is the Tremnor Rol, The Park of Music.

Five bandstands, each large enough for an orchestra, face each other round a shallow amphitheater, sunken into the rock. Each seat on each tier is round, so the listener may turn in any direction best suited to the music. Oh, the concerts on a summer's evening! Sometimes the musicians would be positioned to play parts from different stands, sometimes the work called for different orchestras to play counter to each other. Always all seats were filled, the crowd always loud in its appreciation.

We went together as a family. My father questioned us at breakfast the next morning on what we had heard, on the music's derivations and origins, on the musicians and their pedigree. My sisters would have noticed who was seated near us, who was with whom, what was worn by whom and why.

As I traveled, and my excursions grew more adventurous, I poured over maps of Aleronde. I marveled at her size, at her complexity, at the scale of the planning apparent in her lines and form.

I should say now that the parks are many and in a ring all around the center of Aleronde. One may walk for days and still have more to see. Each is linked with streams and walkways, as I have already described, or with staggered paths, sometimes cut behind a waterfall or curving out over water.

Each park is unique, with its own theme or commemoration. Each is an architectural wonder. Never does the visitor feel that any expense has been spared. All is clean, all is as well cared for as the hall of our house. Each public space is ready, at all times, for the enjoyment of the citizenry. Aleronde The Open! Aleronde The Free!

On one occasion-I was fourteen or fifteen-I was at The Park of Music late after a concert. I had left the family to speak to school friends a few tiers away. My father, thinking I would travel back with my classmates, had taken my siblings home. I had not understood, said good-bye to my friends, and found myself alone in the thinning crowd.

I waited as the stone seats cooled and the air became colder. Soon I was alone. I moved to the top tier and hoped to see my father, or an elder brother, coming over the grass between the bandstands to collect me. No one came.

Eventually, I saw some movement. It was not my family, but the park workers. They came in their hordes, carrying lights and tools, to remove the litter, to cut the grass, to polish the marble, to water or replace the flowers in the beds. I was adrift in a sea of frantic activity. The supervisors had their hands full and did not acknowledge me. Only when most of the work was done did one say to me, "Out late, young sir?"

"True. And amazed at what I see!"

He nodded and replied, "We do our best, sir."

"Indeed so. Tell me, what transport is there at this hour?"

He shook his head, "None that you would wish to take, sir. If you are in need, I will call for help."

I nodded; I had been forgotten and was lacking further resources.

In no time, a police vehicle arrived. I found myself questioned, rudely at first, then allowed aboard. I was not alone. Several others, mostly younger, were also being taken home.

My brothers made much of my adventure the next day. I think my father thought well of me that I had found my own way back, but he made no comment upon it.

The curiosity that flared in me was hard to contain. I had seen a part of my city's life that I had never known-in fact, that I had never suspected. Overnight, our city was renewed! It was transformed from the place I was acquainted with to a factory whose product was cleanliness and order. The workers came, the workers went, and all was well in their wake. I was doubly in love with Aleronde—with its daytime face, of course, and now with its night face. How perfect! How properly ordered! How obvious that such a system would exist in this most excellent of societies!

In my wanderings, I found The Park of Peace, nearest both in distance and spirit to The Port. The architecture is modest, when compared to the parks with commemorative military themes, consisting of low walls engraved with pictures and the sayings of various lands. In pavilions and stalls, carts and around campfires, one can buy foods from every people, from every land. Here the exotic is the norm.

My first visit, one hot day, I watched from a cautious distance the preparation of a strange dish. Above a fiercely flaming fire, in a large shallow metal bowl, a heap of rapidly blackening insects popped and hissed. I turned my head away as I recognized the wings and hooked legs; these were fried Srit-la. The memory of horror from so long in my past had become nothing but an instinctive disgust. I turned my back only to be suddenly transported, transfixed by the smell of a particular spice. It came from the cooking fire of four small workers. To call them ugly would be too kind. Another customer told me they were from Aflunard and their appearance was entirely to be expected. I had half-feared they were the survivors of some dreadful accident, but no, their fathers and their grandfathers also crouched under rounded shoulders and hung their heads to their breasts.

The spice itself, I think, must have been one that the barges brought past our windows in the old house. It captivated me. It flavored a dish that looked bland—a kind of custard I would now say—but once smelled and tasted, could never be forgotten. No dessert, this. A full depth of taste and firm texture led one to take more and more with an enthusiasm its cooks watched with knowing amusement.

The same spice, I heard, is used in a sauce called Marse. But so little is used, it has less of an impact. But in this dish, cooked by those who understood its power, it was unforgettable!

With the smoke from the fires, one did not always appreciate how close one was to The Port. The steams and smokes from the fleet mixed with the cooking and, I should add, with the variety of substances the workers themselves smoked, to make a haze thick enough to hide the comings and goings of several armies.

My brothers told me, after that first visit, I was a fool to go there alone. It was a place with a bad reputation. I could understand why. Amid those clouds and smokes and steams, many an illicit transaction could take place unseen. The workers there often seemed to have no supervisors. Some of the troops coming fresh off the ships too presented a wild appearance and were inclined to trouble.

I went there when I could, though I had to be circumspect with Mother and Father. I rarely came into conflict with any of the people there, being confident in the quickness of my wit as well as, I thought, showing a face that did not brook trouble. But, in the light of more experience, I came to understand I simply posed neither threat nor worthy opportunity.

***

And so, you see me—young, naïve, and a little restless. I bore no ill to anyone—except, in passing, my siblings. I had all of Aleronde to explore. I rejoiced at my fortune that, in all the cosmos, I could live in such a place, at such a time, in such a manner. Of course, soon I would have to turn my hand to gainful employment once my call-up papers came. My father had already laid out that path before my wandering feet.

But for now, I could learn. For me, that learning was to wash in the atmosphere of the city, to walk its paths and parks, to sit by its canals and streams, to eat its foods, to talk late into the night with my peers, and to watch the comings and goings at The Port, for there, at the heart of things, lay the past and the present and the future, wrapped in white steam and black smoke, in familiarity and in mystery.

From: Bookman@____________.co.uk

Subject: Uncle Teddy Comments

Date: Mon, 13 Jun 2011

To: TheoK@_________.com

Hi Theo,

So far the writing is okay, I guess.

Amongst other things, I'm a little puzzled by some omissions Teddy makes. He uses words like "Gre-tra," knowing presumably that they won't translate into English (or he doesn't know how), yet his vocabulary is obviously wide enough that he could have described one. I'm surprised he hasn't given us any clue.

Now I know I complained when we met about some memoirs that have crossed my desk full of "I got up. I cleaned my teeth. I caught the 97 bus to Woolworths to buy socks..." This isn't one of those. But I must warn you, it probably isn't going to fly as is.

Which is why I need to know what we're going to do with it. I have different people who need to be lined up if it's nonfiction or fiction. You see, sometimes, when you've got family sensitivities, fictionalizing a memoir is a good way to go. I'm okay with that.

Since he says he's writing for Marjory, do you have anything from her about him? It might be good for background, if nothing else. Where is this Aleronde? Is he conflating different cities? Where did your family say he came from?

I'll read more when you send it on. He doesn't come over as insane to me.

What do you mean by "the later parts get a bit wild"?

Curt

Email TK 13Jun2011

From: Theo < TheoK@_________.com >

Subject: Re: Uncle Teddy Comments

Date: Mon, 13 Jun 2011

To: Bookman@_____________.co.uk

Curt,

Let's talk about the fact/fiction thing later. Wait until you've seen it all. When you get to the wild bits, you'll see I just mean the later chapters have some odd references. No one in the family had any idea where he actually came from.

As for what a Gre-tra looks like, I know I have a photo somewhere. Patience, and I'll find it. I hear what you say about omissions, but they might not all be Teddy's as such. As I type it up, I'm referencing not only bits of the architecture book and the memoir, but several versions of the memoir, trying to work out what his final intentions were. At the same time, I'm removing stuff that really doesn't make sense. It could be holes in his vocabulary or things he feels he doesn't have to explain, since it's Marjory he's writing to, and maybe she knew a lot of it anyway. I'm doing my best. This isn't your first memoir, but it is mine.

Only Astelle's side of the family talks of insanity seriously. They think one whiff of fruitcake, even of fruitcake-in-law, might spoil the prospects of her appalling brood.

My extended family is truly strange, and I hope you'll be spared having to deal with its outer limits.

As for material from Marjory, I'll look around, but I haven't seen anything in her trunk that fits the bill.

Theo

Chapter Two

Long before my birth, when my father was in his babyhood, our forces and those of the Minfurstiren fought for more than a year. Such a war had never been undertaken before, nor has one so costly befallen us since. The Great Cemetery of Lognor stands in mute and respectful commemoration.

As The Great Parks represent freedom and life for citizens of Aleronde, so too do The Great Cemeteries. Few tears are shed at an Aleronden funeral. Mourning clothes are the same as those for a wedding or a birth. Death and life are not so divided there as they have come to be here.

One spring, one fine and luxuriant spring, I met death and life in Lognor. Sitting on the eastern bank of The Ushnar Canal, Lognor looks across to Quisar, the Park of Catastrophe. Together the park and cemetery form The Mindere, the remembrance of the bloody campaign against the Minfurstiren.

A million men of the Citizen's Army were dead by the end of the campaign. The land of the Minfurstiren, the name of which is never spoken, was laid waste. There are not a million graves, nor even a million arches or plaques in Lognor. Few of the dead returned home.

The paths of the cemetery are long and green, the walls low and modest. At regular intervals new paths curve off the main way and curl into small hidden gardens, surrounded by hedges or well-groomed trees. In some gardens there are fountains, in others, columns with names etched with small deep cuts. It is a place of silence, of memory, of facing our collective destiny, and of realizing the costs of being Aleronde The Magnificent.

Let me say more about the spring, for the contrast with the late winter in Aleronde is as great as day and night. The last snows drift in and turn to rain. The ice on the canals retreats to cling to the walls and banks. For a week, perhaps longer, all is silent.

The migrating birds come on the south wind with a rising clamor, heard for a day before they arrive to cover the budding trees, strut on the lawns, or fight for purchase on the green and blue tiled roofs.

All feel the coming of spring. My mother would sing at the top of her voice as she pursued her team of houseworkers, driving them into a blur of activity. Even my father would smile as he looked out of his office windows at the emergence of vivid blooms, the closing in of the trees, the transformation of the landscape before the house.

You must put this seasonal eruption of life in the context of my late adolescence. I walked in Lognor, feeling the new year's life twine its energy up from the ground through my feet and into my legs and chest. My shoulders were hot from the sun, my eyes bright. I took a curving detour into one of the gardens.

I never knew her name, nor she mine. We both felt the power of the spring. She too had wandered through Lognor, in search of memories—memories of people who had gone even before we drew breath.

She asked me if I were a soldier, like those recalled around us.

"Not yet," I replied. That was the truth, for my papers had yet to arrive.

"Where are you from?" I asked her.

"Garton," she said, and I understood at once.

Garton was a place of desperation, a place of last resort, for families blighted by war, for children orphaned and unclaimed, girls left without guardians. They all came to reside at Garton.

"You lost much," I said.

"My grandparents. My mother lived there. I was born there."

I looked around. "Then this is your true home. This is where your family is."

She nodded. "More here than anywhere else. It is rare to meet a man who understands that."

We sat in silence for a long time. She took my hand and said, "I feel the year change. Celebrate with me."

My first thought was that we would have to walk a long way for refreshments. It was not what she meant.

Her hands were warm but rough-skinned, I guessed, from manual labor. I'm sure I did not impress her with my early fumblings but we were soon overtaken by sweeping sensations of physical love.

Our nakedness under the sky was one with the sunshine, the birdsong, the budding and blooming. The transformation in the air was echoed and replayed. My body felt reborn. I was a reptile shedding its skin. I was dawn breaking.

Of course, I was also crossing a line for which my parents would probably have had me exiled. Happily, no such concerns troubled us that unforgettable afternoon in spring.

***

I went back to find the garden, to find her, my Goddess of Spring, the next week. She was not there. My eagerness was rewarded only after a month. Alas, that month had brought other changes.

I have not yet told you of one of my older brothers; Hal-fi was his name. Yes, his living story has ended and he has taken his place among the dead.

In all our games and fighting in the house, in all the debates around the table, Hal-fi was fair to me. He was not generous, he was not kind, but fairness he chose with deliberation.

Hal-fi was not the eldest, not to be our father's heir. That fell rather to Rol-di, who even groomed himself to appear like Father. Father taught him to command. That was his position and he wore it well, though we all knew he was neither Father's nor our intellectual equal.

But as for Hal-fi, if I say he excelled at everything, you'll think me sentimental and that my memory is clouded. But truly, he excelled at all he put his hand to. He became the youngest captain in his regiment. He was appointed the youngest general in the army's history. He played music with a proficiency I envy still. The glamorous and the rich and the powerful all came when it was announced he would take a wife. Our father had no want of candidates.

The parties and the entertaining went on for months. We were all on our best behavior—even our sisters, who would have died rather than miss the parade of Aleronde's finest young women dressed to capture our brother's heart. We wondered, each of us, if we would have such a panorama of choice when our turn came to marry.

Then, overshadowing the wedding, came news of the Chogren. I had never heard of them, nor had any of my contemporaries. They had attacked a diplomatic mission. They set themselves in opposition to Aleronde. Hal-fi was placed in charge of our response.

He came home injured. No one would tell us what had happened.

The house was in turmoil. Hal-fi was taken into one of Mother's rooms along with such a wealth of medical equipment that we shook our heads in hopelessness. Doctors of all kinds visited. Even medical workers from other lands were called, in case their expertise could offer any benefit.

Two weeks were all we had with him before he died. For much of that time he was in a delirium, thrashing to flee imagined or, perhaps, remembered foes. My father retreated in grief, and we saw him little. Mother stood firm, on watch with Hal-fi's new wife, day and night until lack of sleep forced her too to withdraw.

I had one conversation with him during a lucid period.

"Do not doubt," was his message to me. "Don't look with fear at what has happened to me. Look to the empire and its glory. There is no other place like this, no other people our betters. Be proud. Be strong."

I came to understand this was his message to each of his brothers in turn.

Two days after his death, papers came instructing that my time in service would begin. Matters with the Chogren were still outstanding. I presumed I would be in a position in some small way to avenge the loss of my brother. I felt ready.

With this then turning my world around, I went once more to the cemetery in search of my Spring Goddess. In the garden I found only a girl, the same girl from Garton. She knew at once I had been called. The stone of the memorials reflected in our eyes.

We made love, not as minor deities, but as a lonely boy and lonelier girl. I felt not the change from winter to spring, or from spring to summer, but the onset of a winter I was afraid might not end.

"I will pray for you," she said, "I will come here, each month, and wait for your return."

It was my first test of courage. I wanted her to do neither but was too much a coward to say so. I nodded and left her surrounded by the birdsong and her ancestors.

From: Bookman@____________.co.uk

Subject: Uncle Teddy Question

Date: Tue, 14 Jun 2011

To: TheoK@_________.com

Hi Theo,

Do I understand that you are editing this stuff before sending it?

Please don't.

I have editors to do that for you—you know, they edit things, they're good at it. Really, they have a more experienced eye for what will make the story work, and what might be fluff.

Let me have it all. Let me see what I'm dealing with.

Curt

From the Desk of
Curtis Bookman

Nancy,
Re: Kingman Memoir

Please prepare the following:
Letter to Prof. John Warren,
______ College, Oxford, marked
Private and Confidential.
Send copies of Chapters 1 and 2.
Ask if he recognizes the place names,
etc.

over...

Letter to Prof. Eric Campbell,
______ College, Cambridge,
marked Private and Confidential.
Send copies of Chapter 1 and 2.
Ask if he recognizes anything at all.

Curt

Mrs. P. Kingman

The Grange

Middle Uffet

Gloucestershire

30 June 2011

Dear Sirs,

It has come to our attention that certain writings of a private nature have come into your possession, purporting to be the memoirs of a member of this family.

We trust that a firm in such good standing as yours will not be proceeding with these documents until the following matters are resolved.

THE MANUSCRIPT'S PROVENANCE. Various claims are made as to the history thereof. We urge you not to take seriously the frivolous claims you may have heard to date.

THE WORK'S AUTHENTICITY. We are sure by now you have come to wonder whether those passing off this manuscript as a true memoir are being honest with you. They are not.

THE WORK'S IMPACT. Do not think this family will sit idle while its name is held up to ridicule by association with this false memoir. We will defend our good name by all necessary means.

Yours sincerely,

Mrs. P. Kingman

Mrs. P. Kingman

The Village Pub

Small Community Publishing

____

London, _________

5 July 2011

Dear Mrs. Kingman,

Thank you for your most interesting letter concerning your brother-in-law's memoir.

As I am sure you are aware, I have the final word on all books that bear our imprint.

I wish to address each of your concerns in turn.

Provenance – You describe the presenters' claims as frivolous, but offer no counterclaim.

Authenticity – Under this heading, you cast doubt upon the honesty of the presenters, rather than on the matter of authorship. I take this to be a tacit admission that your brother-in-law Teddy is the actual author. Thank you.

Impact – I presume this is intended as a threat. Please consider carefully which would be more detrimental to your family's good name: a memoir, or the failure of a lawsuit attempting to suppress the legitimate publication of the memoir.

I will be deciding whether to publish this, as I do any book, on the grounds of its intrinsic merit, its future sales potential, and the state of the current market. If you have any substantive information that may help my decision, I would ask you please to come forward with it as soon as possible.

Yours sincerely,

Curt Bookman

From: Bookman@_____________.co.uk

Subject: Uncle Teddy

Date: Tue, 05 Jul 2011

To: TheoK@_________.com

Theo,

The cat is out of the bag. Had a threatening letter from Mrs. P. Kingman. Am I right presuming that's Astelle?

She knows we have the manuscript and is not pleased.

I guess they know you're working on it? Have they been threatening you too?

Curt

Email TK 05Jul2011

From: Theo < TheoK@_________.com >

Subject: Re: Uncle Teddy

Date: Tue, 05 Jul 2011

To: Bookman@_____________.co.uk

Ooops.

Thanks for the warning.

Yes, they've been at me for a while. A heavy even turned up at the house. I'm happy to say my two Great Danes expressed keen interest in playing with him.

I actually have a secret lair. I didn't think I'd have to retreat to it quite so soon ;-)

Theo

From: JW < John_Warren@__________.ox.ac.uk >

Subject: Re: Request from Curt Bookman

Date: Wed, 06 Jul 2011

To: Bookman@______________.co.uk

Curt,

Thanks for sharing the material, I think.

What a pig's ear! Where did you get it?

I presume it's been translated (mostly). Any idea from what?

JW

Email CB 07Jul2011

From: Bookman@_____________.co.uk

Subject: JW

Date: Thu, 07 Jul 2011

To: TheoK@_________.com

Theo,

Remember JW? I ran into him recently and showed him a few pages. Hope you don't mind. He has become *the* expert on linguistics. Thought it might be useful.

He wondered if this version was a translation. If so, from what and by whom?

Curt

From: Theo < TheoK@_________.com >

Subject: Re: JW

Date: Fri, 08 Jul 2011

To: Bookman@_____________.co.uk

Curt,

Of course I remember JW. Haven't spoken to him in years.

Yes, he's spot on.

Q1. The answer is attached.

Q2. Teddy.

Looks like he wrote it all like this and then used it as an exercise in practicing English. He did it a couple of times over, judging by the different drafts I have.

As for your telling me off for editing rather than have your people do it – I've been through it all several times, so I already know that some of the early passages are best moved to later. We'll talk it over once you get the rest.

I got intrigued by Uncle Teddy's story when I read those pages I handed you when we met. Some of what he describes seems so strange – dreamlike almost – and some seems so familiar, don't you think?

Theo

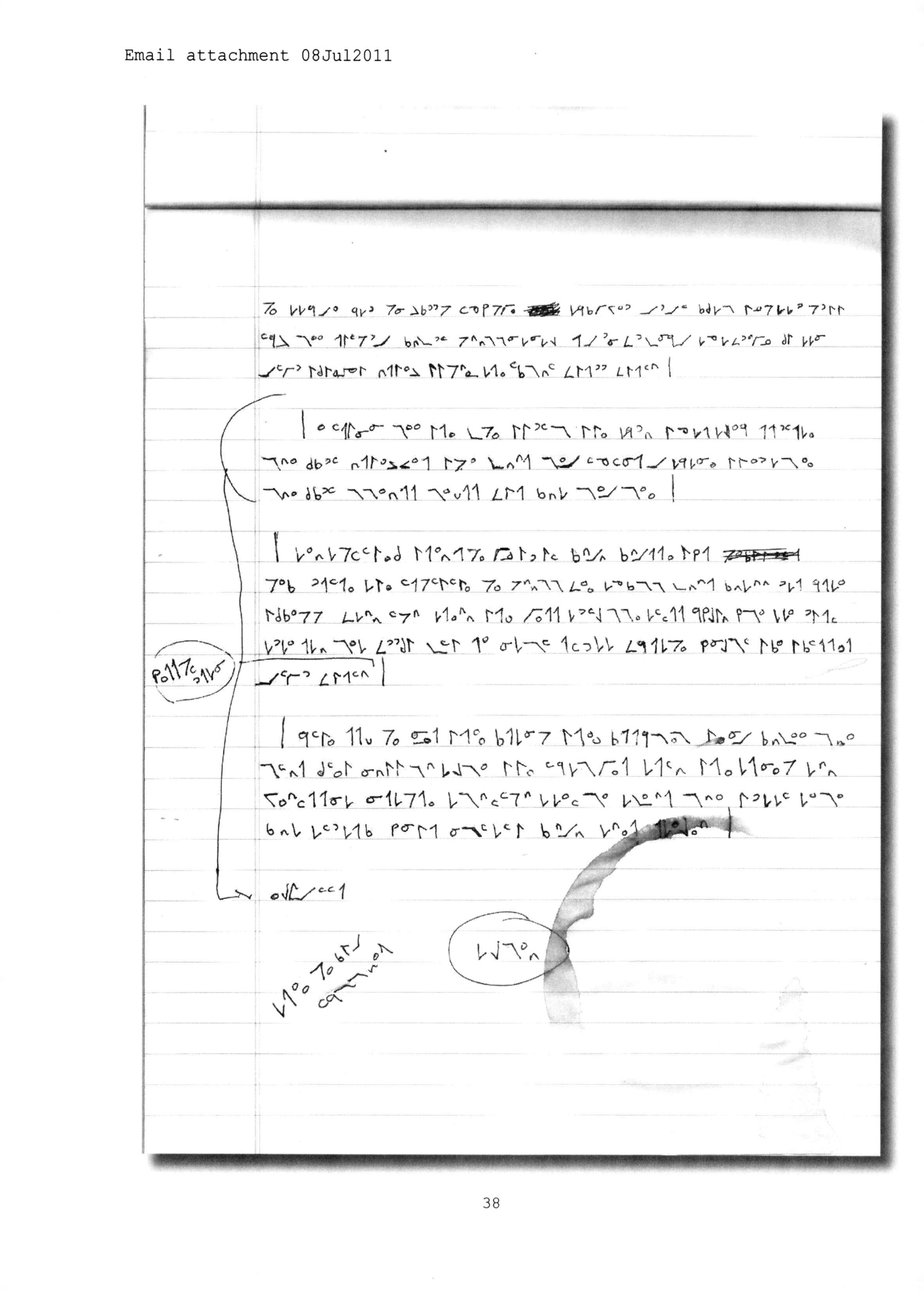

Email EC 12Jul2011

From: Eric Campbell < CampbellEric@_________.cam.ac.uk >

Subject: Re: Request from Curt Bookman

Date: Tue, 12 Jul 2011

To: Bookman@_____________.co.uk

Dear Curt,

I have examined the pages you sent. I understand you were hoping for a location or an indication of a period.

Unfortunately, I cannot oblige. There is not enough detail or context.

The nearest I can relate to this sort of description is the sort of guff that comes up every decade or so when some nutcase sphinx-hugger comes off a UFO encounter claiming to have been to The Hidden City.

My advice is throw it away.

Eric

From the Desk of
Curtis Bookman

Re: Kingman Memoir

Nancy,

I said <u>letters</u> to John Warren and Eric Campbell for a reason.

Why am I getting email replies from them?

Written letters are more private nowadays.

Curt

From the Desk of
Nancy Worth

Re: Kingman memoir

Sorry, I'm obviously addicted to the wonders of modern technology. You know we retired the remaining quill pen last week ;-)

N.

P.S. From what I've read of this one, G.C.H.Q. aren't going to care.

Email JW 12Jul2011

From: JW < John_Warren@_________.ox.ac.uk >

Subject: Re: Further Information from Curt Bookman

Date: Tue, 12 Jul 2011

To: Bookman@_____________.co.uk

Curt,

Thanks for the sample but no, no, and no!

Where did you get this stuff?

Tell me this is real and I'd have to have a team of post-docs risking careers on it.

But, no, this can't be anything but a fake. I just hope you didn't lay out an advance on this one!

JW

From: Bookman@____________.co.uk

Subject: Uncle Teddy

Date: Tue, 12 Jul 2011

To: TheoK@________.com

Okay, Theo, JW has spoken.

I showed him the funny page you sent. He doesn't believe it.

That means I don't either.

Talk to me.

Curt

Email TK 14Jul2011

From: Theo < TheoK@__________.com >

Subject: Re: Uncle Teddy

Date: Thu, 14 Jul 2011

To: Bookman@_____________.co.uk

Dear Curt,

You're only the publisher; you don't have to believe it! ;-) I really wanted your own unfiltered take on it – that's why I specifically asked you in the first place not to show it to anyone else. Oh well.

I wonder if JW will remember the park? Did you show him that section too?

Here are some letters I found in my mother's things. They're addressed to Grandma Doris, (Marjory calls her Sis, though they were in-laws.) They must have been quite close. I didn't realize my mother had kept anything like this and didn't realize who they were from until I started reading.

I've put off going through my parents' effects for almost ten years now. The accident was difficult enough. I put everything in storage; the journey through Aunt Marjory's things was so much easier. Moving myself to avoid the attentions of Astelle has had its benefits, I suppose – I found these!

It's so frustrating that we don't have the other half of the correspondence. There weren't any letters at all in Marjory's trunk. Grandma never talked about all this (to me anyway) but you and I would have been what – fifteen? – when she died in '92.

Attached also is the next chapter. This is the military bit. It gets weirder from here.

Theo

The Residence

1 May 1960

Dear Sis,

Thanks for the flowers. They brighten the room wonderfully.

I'm snowed under at the moment. I have two men brought back from Malaya at the end of last year. One has old-fashioned shell shock; the other is falling asleep the whole time. I've no idea what to do for him, poor fellow!

But I have another patient who is somewhat different. He's an amnesiac but isn't showing the typical symptoms. He's more like a foreigner who took a wrong turn. I also think he's been wrongly classified; they have him in lockdown.

The thing is I think I might be falling for him. I know, as unprofessional as it gets! Send more chocolates...

M.

The Residence
8 May 1960

Dear Sis,

Thanks a lot! And no, as you know quite well, amnesiacs aren't any sort of Unitarian!

I'm serious. And he is really good-looking. No, he's actually handsome, in the sense that "good-looking" is only skin-deep.

Apart from the rules about relationships with patients, I don't think there's a problem... You're right, vulnerable people can be manipulative. I know that and can see it a mile off. In fact, most men on a first date can be too. This one isn't like that.

Half my time with him is spent teaching him English. He's a quick study, which lends more weight to him being high functioning, despite the underlying trauma.

I really want to get him out of this place as soon as I can. I don't think the orderlies like him much. They seem wary of him. I'll talk with Dr. Beech next Friday. Maybe I can recommend some day passes.

Keep your fingers crossed that this doesn't backfire on me.

M.

The Residence

23 May 1960

Dear Sis,

I got Teddy out into the park yesterday. You should have seen his face! I wish I could have taken a photo of that grin — ear to ear!

Dr. Beech is still cautious. I probably shouldn't write this, but it seems there was some trouble when Teddy was first admitted. He shows no sign of it now. So, don't worry!!

My main concern is to get him transferred to another therapist, then my ethical problems go away. I can keep on with the English lessons privately.

M.

The Residence

30 May 1960

No, Sis, "English Lessons" isn't a codeword. He is very much a gentleman!

What can I tell you about him?

Teddy has some odd political reactions. He's a bit sensitive about class matters and who works for whom and under what conditions. I wonder if he was in a bad situation in his former life.

Learning another language seems something completely new and fascinating for him. The funny thing is, he's a natural. Most people have trouble learning their first foreign tongue as adults.

He really wants to travel, seems interested in forests and zoos, old buildings, and military commemorations. We passed a statue of some general on a horse – you've seen it, the one by the duck pond? – he wanted me to tell him the whole story. I hadn't a clue! I'll have to get him a library card.

Teddy is exhausting in that he gets enthusiastic serially. He opens a box and is transported with wonder until he opens a new box more fascinating than the first.

My one worry – okay, one of my worries – is when he tells me things about his past. Many trauma victims retreat into a coping fantasy to explain the inexplicable or the unbearable – especially young ones. Kids will say that parents are away visiting relatives when they know their parents are dead.

But Teddy is, of course, different. His persistent fantasy account of his memory loss is to do with a cave and a beautiful city where he once lived. I've never heard of a fantasy so detailed and tenacious. When he talks about it, he gets a look in his eye like a religious devotion.

I wonder how we can ever hope to cure him of it. I wonder how I can ever hope to compete with it.

M.

The Residence

15 Jun 1960

Dear Sis,

Thanks for the advice. No, realistically now I don't think we'll ever know about the origins of his fantasy world. And, no, we still have no clue where he actually came from. They had several tries at identifying his writing and his speech, but nothing.

The science only takes you so far. At some point you say, "This is it. We move on with what we have."

I'd like to bring him to dinner. Will Saturday be okay?

M.

The Residence

18 June 1960

Dear Sis,

Yes, I have thought (quite a lot) what would happen if he remembers he's already married. (But I don't think he was a criminal.)

I could deal with it. Let's face it, Sis, my clock is ticking. I'm a professional woman, a therapist, and men find me intimidating. Teddy doesn't. That matters to me.

Saturday week it is then.

Love you,

M.

The Residence

2 July 1960

Dear Sis,

I'm so glad you and Robert got along so well with Teddy. Isn't he wonderful? You're right, his appetite is amazing, I've noticed that before.

And again you're right — I hadn't thought of what Astelle will think! It'll do her good to have something worth worrying about - a real unknown quantity in the family!

As I've said before, I'm not inclined to let our beloved sister-in-law have any say in what I do. Poor Peter, but then as we say, his choice.

Come and visit. We'll take Teddy to the zoo. He can practice his taxonomic vocabulary on you.

I love Robert's idea of getting him part-time work (my brother can be quite insightful when he has a mind to be). Teddy needs social experiences, and having some money of his own would be therapeutic too.

From the way they got so involved in talking about photography, he seems to know quite a lot already, so it's a good fit.

Love,

M.

The Residence

21 September 1960

Dear Sis,

He's decided on keeping "Smith." I told him why he, like every other unknown person in England, was called that when he was admitted. He told me all about blacksmiths. That library has a lot to answer for!

So, John Smith is now legally Teddy Smith.

And I've agreed to be Marjory Smith!

He popped the question this morning. I'd only opened your letter warning me he was going to ask me about ten minutes before! I didn't have time to really compose myself, but at least I had taken a couple of long breaths. Thanks!

How typical of Teddy to write to Robert. Was he asking permission? Did he really ask the best way to propose? I'm sure he did a lot more research besides!

We'll show you the ring at the weekend. We should be there for lunch.

Love,

M.

Chapter Three

Basic training was less trouble than school. My excitement at starting officer orientation flared and died in the mind-numbing presence of the desiccated corpse lecturing us. After a young life hearing of the glory of military service and the skill and acumen of our brave souls in uniform, I suspected it was a deliberate exercise to lower our expectations.

I was, as a new officer without experience, given charge of ten soldiers, also new and without experience. My commander assured me privately our assignments would be commensurate with our skills. This too succeeded in lowering our expectations.

We gathered, our training accomplished and our hopes duly trimmed, at The Port.

I have mentioned The Port lies within the circle of The Great Parks. It sprawls over an area proportionate to the left cheek of the face of the city. It does not behoove one to become lost once inside.

I traveled, in the company of hundreds of new recruits and officers, from the northern entrance along narrow roads, walled with goods coming in and goods going out to the far reaches of the empire. At intersections, I briefly caught sight of stretches of worker housing or, in the distance—and at one glorious moment up close—a huge ship readying to depart. I swung rapidly from an aching boredom to the hot flush of an excitement not felt since childhood and then back again just as quickly.

When I let it, the thought that I was to walk aboard one of these monsters and travel to the colonies and beyond became dizzying. Thoughts of exotic forests filled my mind.

We waited, ate, and slept in a warehouse for three days before seeing our ship. Vendors of foreign foods that I recognized from The

Park of Peace did endless business. The impressive size of the room did not save us from the smell of new food; old food; smoke; unwashed bodies; and, as time dragged on and the warehouse filled, more bodies.

I lay for long hours against my bags wondering about the girl from Garton, imagining what my siblings were doing, listening in my mind to the last concert I heard at the Tremnor Rol.

I knew the ship was ready when I attended a small ceremony at which I was assigned a Gre-tra.

My Gre-tra would be my helper, my servant, my constant companion while in service. I think, at first sight of each other, neither of us welcomed the thought. My father had always told me how such employment ennobled these primitive people. I reluctantly took up my duty to see to the ennobling of this one.

"Your name?" I asked.

"Allo." The word hung in the air. The depth of the lack of enthusiasm with which he spoke his own name made me sad.

"Have you served an officer before?"

He nodded slowly.

"What happened to him?"

"Five. All killed. All in battle, never come back."

I wasn't sure how to reply, but I was certain humor would be wasted. At least he would know what to do, how to arrange my quarters, keep my uniform straight, wake me at the appropriate times.

"Good, Allo! It is my intention to live. I expect you to do your part in making that so."

Allo nodded again, slowly, and said nothing.

We settled into a small berth next to a larger one. In the larger was my troop. I watched Allo unpack and neatly store my gear. I studied the diagram of the ship. That we were close to the mess hall on our deck was good news. We were less close to the showers; that was bad news. I waited a long time before I went next door to introduce myself.

They were noisy—ten of them sounded like forty. I opened the door; the first one to see me, and the insignia at my breast, swore loudly and hid something smoking behind his back. The others quickly stood, bolt upright and silent.

It was my first real lesson in leadership; I smelled their fear.

"Stand easy," I said into the silence.

There was an exhaling of smoky breath.

I looked around at the faces and said, "Whatever that is you're smoking, make sure you have some left for the journey back. You might need it."

They shared surprised glances.

"Oh," I continued, "and be ready two minutes before meal call. I mean ready to run. We're nearer than most to the mess hall, but I want to be there first. Understood?"

"Yes, Sir!" they replied as one. I think one or two of them even smiled.

"That's all. We'll introduce ourselves properly later. Relax while you can."

I left them to wonder what sort of lunatic had been put in charge of them.

The journey was strangely timeless in the confines of the bare rooms and corridors. My main task each day seemed to be the breaking up of fights among my men or between them and other troops. Time spent hauling my brothers off each other was bearing fruit.

One pleasant surprise awaited me as we jostled in line one day at the mess. Another troop leader punched me in the shoulder and gave a cheery shout.

His name was Mer-fo; we'd known one another when we were very young, before his family moved to another part of Aleronde. And here he was, commanding a similar group of unlikely soldiers, on the same mission.

Like me, he had been in the warehouse, received his Gre-tra, had been likewise bored to the point of insanity, yet we had never spotted each other. We made up for lost time during the journey.

Eventually, we attended our mission briefing. As I left for it, even Allo seemed uncomfortable.

Our orders were simple: to secure buildings already cleared by more hardened soldiers as they expanded our occupation of the Chogren city called Axequap. Good enough work for new soldiers. There was limited danger from the enemy and limited opportunity for my men to be a danger to themselves.

***

I addressed my men: "We will be transported to an area of buildings that have been cleared of indigenous occupants. We will go building to building and ensure they are empty. There exists the possibility of saboteurs remaining in hiding.

"We will enter each building in pairs. I will accompany each pair in turn-so you will have me watching you! You will check every crawl space, every cupboard, every loose cover. You will kill anything you find alive. When and if you do so, you will retreat from the building immediately. Assume any living presence renders the entire building unsafe. You will mark the entryway with this tape."

I held up a roll of bright orange tape. "This will signify to all that the building is unsafe and mark it for destruction. I say again, anything living is to be killed immediately. Questions?"

Mal-gi, who turned out to be one of the two bright men in my troop, asked, "Can you tell us anything about the Chogren?"

Before I could answer, one of the others, Tre-hu, said, "He wants to know if the females are fuckable!"

As the laughter died down I said, "The Chogren are like us, I hear. But they are the enemy. Our mission is to kill any we find." I pointed at Tre-hu's groin. "You will be issued a weapon more effective than that to kill them with."

Again the laughter. I thought it healthy—better to laugh than to think of opportunities to die.

"One more thing." I held up a collection sack. "Each team will be issued one of these. You will place in here any objects of a technological nature you find. Anything useful, anything you don't recognize. Anything. Our engineers are waiting to examine all the devices we bring back. Anything too large to carry gets dragged out to the front of the building. Now..." I looked them all in the eye. "As to the matter of things you intend putting in your pockets..."

All eyes looked to the floor. I had been briefed that new troops often competed in collecting trinkets and inevitably returned with dangerous souvenirs. I sighed. "Look. I'm not going to tell you not to bring back anything. Be sensible. Nothing organic. Absolutely nothing alive! If I find you have something in your pocket that we don't also have in the sack, there'll be trouble. Also, it's our first time doing this. I don't want competition among ourselves. This is how we'll work it: everything that comes back here, not in a sack, gets shared. We put it all out on the table here and divide it up. We work for each other. Any objections?"

There were none, only that look again as though they had a lunatic for an officer. I thought, *So be it.*

***

We were all shaken to the bone by the ride to our mission zone. The door dropped and we hit foreign soil at a run. The air smelled of smoke, burnt meat, and spilled fuel. The light was bright, the sun hot. A Situation Commander met us, shouting orders over the roar of the vehicles. This, of course, was not what I had hoped for in traveling to foreign lands. But too much was happening too quickly for me to dwell upon it.

As directed, we began our search at the corner of the street ahead of us. The buildings were low, only one or two levels, plain and ugly, and fashioned from some sort of clay brick, assembled with a modicum of skill in lines that were level and clean-edged. That the buildings had no glass in the windows may have been attributable to the action of our own forces. I saw no trees and only a few burnt plants.

I pointed my teams to the nearest five buildings and followed the first pair into the corner house. We were cautious, of course, but in fact, we could not move fast. The floors were strewn with broken furniture, glass, torn fabrics, and pieces of fallen ceiling.

We slipped our heat-sensitive filters over our visors. I could hardly believe it when, on climbing to the first upper level, we saw a faint glow behind a cupboard door.

We stood shoulder-to-armored-shoulder, raised our weapons, and blew the cupboard and its occupant out of the side of the building.

All three of us were giddy with excitement. I had to shout the orders to move carefully back out of the house and put the tape up over the entrance.

House to house, shop to shop, we found no other heat signatures. The adrenaline burst of that first encounter kept all of us feeling tall and powerful—until I lost a team.

They entered the last building at the next intersection. I was inside a small house with another team, three houses away. The killing blast dislodged the ceiling on top of us.

The Situation Commander was stern faced; I could tell he had seen it all before. The ambulance crew efficiently retrieved the corpses. The remaining teams carried on. I joined one in a larger house.

This house was less damaged than the others. There were no heat signatures, so I sat in a chair while the other two finished checking. Next to me was a pile of rubbish. Sticking out from it was a book.

Still wearing my reinforced gloves, I dusted off the plain cloth cover. Its pages were square and heavy, and each bore a single image of a Chogren family. In the images, I recognized the rooms of the house in which I sat. A family, some four children and parents and perhaps the grandparents, smiled for the camera. In one picture, a celebration; in another a child wearing a colorful hat; some sort of special meal; a child hugging an animal, ugly, small, and hairy.

Now understand, I had no sympathy for this family, for who else would make up the forces of the enemy than individuals who lived in family groups? No, my concern was far deeper, far more disturbing. I cannot truly express the horror that overcame me. I can only hint at it and hope you will understand. My world was shaken, my heart beating fast, not with the thrill of a kill but with fear.

The images were colorful!

They were not paintings; I knew they were photographs. I could even see the effects of a flash gun held a little too close to the subject. But neither were they photographs that had been artificially colored. They were alive with natural colors, as the eye sees them!

For me, a photograph was always an image made of white, gray, and black, though sometimes, instead, it might have a brown cast from the developing chemicals. Never had I seen or heard of a camera that could capture natural colors. I thought about the objects we had seen in the houses and shops. Nowhere had we seen a camera plate, nor a tripod, no light chambers or hoods. How had these Chogren created these images? And why, being able to perform such a feat, would they waste it on such trivia as I saw before me?

I only brought one object back to the ship, the book of colorful photographs. It scared me to the roots of my being.

The eight others returned with their sacks full of odd devices, and their pockets full of mysterious finds. There was what might have been Chogren currency, some personal jewelry of metal and glittering stones, some small technological devices sufficiently common to have already been adequately represented in the sacks.

The dividing of our spoils was not the celebration we had anticipated. Two empty bunks took the joy from our treasures. I soon withdrew to the company of Allo, in his solemn silence, a presence more appropriate to my mood than sitting in company and smoking an hallucinogen.

***

In the days that followed, I lost no more men, but too many of our neighbors on board did not return. The mission zones extended further and further from the ship. The excitement at a kill lessened. Each new street was more routine, and we lost interest in souvenirs. I looked for no more books of photographs. One was enough.

Then one clear, smokeless day, at the end of a Chogren street of mixed businesses and housing, we stood before a large structure, perhaps a meeting hall or performance space. I watched as Mer-fo took his team in.

Immediately, two Chogren fighters ran from a rear door, as an explosion roared and the floor collapsed. Within moments, Mer-fo and his troop, all eleven, were dead. The enemy killed seven more of us in the street outside.

The treacherous nature of the Chogren tactics was beyond my understanding. That my friend, so newly rediscovered, should fall in such a way wrenched my heart.

***

This Chogren city was taken and entirely cleared. Eventually all Chogren cities would be taken, the surviving population, portion by portion, removed to camps where their true skills could be assessed.

At the end of our tour, before our ship turned for home, I sat at dinner with all the officers on board. The captain stood and, in an uncharacteristic display of eloquence, summarized our experiences in only three sentences.

"We have encountered our hostile neighbors. Their weapons were useless, their resistance futile. They will now take their rightful place in the good order of the Empire."

We replied as one, "Aleronde The Great! Aleronde The Feared! Aleronde The Magnificent!"

My fist pumped the air, but my heart did not rise. I was cold with doubt. The Chogren, the makers of colorful photographs, would do so no longer. They would be given other work to do and somehow I counted that a loss. For my fallen soldiers' sake, and for that of Mer-fo, I could feel no sympathy for any of the Chogren fighters, who I knew to be treacherous and dishonorable opponents. Yet, on a greater scale, I suspected we had inadvertently broken something, perhaps something precious. It was a confusion for which I was unprepared. How could I hate the Chogren and yet wish we had met them in peace?

I could not share the enthusiasm of the others for returning home. I was wary of rejoining my family. I now understood why, so often, returning soldiers wore a wild and troubled countenance. How could one hide such deep doubts, such a shaking of one's world? I knew I could not. I resolved to speak to no one until I had addressed these matters with both Mother and Father-no matter the consequences.

To say that Allo understood would be to attribute too much to my servant, but his manner was appropriate to my state of mind. I was glad never to be alone. Each night he took his place on the floor at the foot of my bed. He said little, showed no joy in life, greeted each day with the same baleful eyes. I had unraveled the objections I had to him at our first meeting. He was my ideal Gre-tra.

From the Desk of
Nancy Worth

Re: Kingman memoir

I'm reading the latest dose. The relationship with his valet is bloody peculiar. What is he, a slave!?!

People aren't going to like this as written.

N.

By Certified Mail

Mr. Thomas A. Ernest QC

Ernest and Ernest

Ernest House

__________ Street

London SW1

19 July 2011

Dear Sirs,

I have been contacted by Mrs. Astelle Kingman in regard to the putative memoir of her late brother-in-law.

Please understand that I will personally be dealing with any litigation that may arise from any attempt to publish this work.

I would advise you to drop all such plans immediately. As far as I can see from my initial review, you have no legal grounds and would surely lose if the matter were ever to be brought to court.

Yours sincerely,

T. A. E.

From the Desk of
Curtis Bookman

Re: Ernest letter

Nancy,
Please frame this and hang it in the Rogue's Gallery.

Curt

From the Desk of
Nancy Worth

Re: Kingman memoir

Ellie and I were talking. He describes The Port as being huge – a cheek on the face of the city – yet The Parks go around outside The Port. What kind of port goes inside of a city? I definitely smell something fishy. Have you decided yet if we are having the wool pulled?

N.

Email CB 25Jul2011

From: Bookman@_____________.co.uk

Subject: Current Project

Date: Mon, 25 Jul 2011

To: TheoK@_________.com

Did you get my voice messages? Our offices were broken into last night. They got all the computers, backup drives and your papers.

Please resend materials. We're at my place until we get the office set up again.

Are you safe?

Curt

Email TK 25Jul2011

From: Theo < TheoK@_________.com >

Subject: Re: Current Project

Date: Mon, 25 Jul 2011

To: Bookman@_____________.co.uk

Yes, got your messages. Thanks. Sorry to hear this. I didn't think they'd stoop quite that low.

I'm keeping the stuff and myself safe. So far so good.

Did the QC threaten you yet? I have a stack of embossed letterhead from him. Such a bullshitter.

Theo

Email BL 27Jul2011

From: Bob < BobL@__________-investigations.com >

Subject: Starbucks

Date: Wed, 27 Jul 2011

To: Bookman@______________.co.uk

Mr. Bookman, despite what I said to you in Starbucks, I can't take the case. Looks like your thiefs got friends in serious high places. They already leaned on me. From that I can tell you for free they got someone following you.

Divorces and missing cats is my business, can't afford that kind of grief. Sorry.

Bob

From: Bookman@____________.co.uk

Subject: Current Project

Date: Tue, 02 Aug 2011

To: TheoK@_________.com

Theo,

Thanks for the new copies. As you can tell, the new PCs are up and running.

You know I'm in your corner as far as Astelle and her QC go, but please understand, I am having doubts. You're still editing, aren't you?

I was about to go round the academics to try and identify the war, but I held off. I should warn you, among the juniors, reading all this has become something of an office sport.

Infrared visors, but no color photos.

Servants treated like slaves in this day and age.

Really?

And you're editing/hiding some of the things he writes about.

So I'm thinking maybe Astelle is correct and Uncle Teddy was insane.

Are there any other ways you take after him?

Curt

Email TK 02Aug2011

From: Theo < TheoK@_________.com >

Subject: Re: Current Project

Date: Tue, 02 Aug 2011

To: Bookman@_____________.co.uk

Attached again are those first few pages I started with.

It's where he describes the triangular park. This is why I first got really interested in Uncle Teddy and his book.

Please have a close read of them again. Really, read closely. You said originally that you remembered being there.

Thanks, and though I realize this is causing more grief than we first thought it might, I know you'll find it's worth it in the end.

Theo

From: Bookman@____________.co.uk

Subject: Re: Current Project

Date: Wed, 03 Aug 2011

To: TheoK@_________.com

Ok. I read them again.

I already knew it was off the Edgware Road. It's round from my Aunt Violet's. (She of the Uncle of the Month, remember?) You stayed with me there a couple of times before term started.

One of the warehouse buildings belonged to a printer. Remember raiding bins for misprinted trading cards? I wonder now if that's how I got interested in printing and publishing?

Anyway, I probably had my journal going then. I hate looking back through that.

Curt

From: Theo < TheoK@_________.com >

Subject: Re: Current Project

Date: Wed, 03 Aug 2011

To: Bookman@_____________.co.uk

In the words of a publisher friend of mine, "Talk to me."

Theo

The Village Pub
Small Community Publishing

London, __________

6 August 2011

Dear Theo,

The password for yesterday's thumb-drive is

Uncle-Teddy__is=insane+

Nancy assures me this will work. What do I know?

It seems a lot of fuss for five files.

Curt

—Theo, Here are pages from my journal.

First one was long ago. We were about 9.
Second was long ago too, but slightly less so.

Third wasn't so long ago. I've had this dream many times. I didn't really need to look this one up, I remember it vividly.

Dream last night.
There was a bus. Edgware Rd, I think.
No one on it except me and Auntie V.
Wandered down a grassy bank into the park
round the corner. Weirdo place in the daytime,
worse at night.
Dead rosebush in a bed full of cigarette ends.
Then the cave. Before I went in I turned
around and looked back to the grassy bank
and saw the lights of traffic going by. Hardly
heard the noise. Everything seemed muffled.

The cave was really dark.
Smelled damp. Sudden loud gongs and whistles.
Woke up when the dog barked.

Dream. Staying at Auntie Violet's
Ran down the grassy bank, straight over to the cave.
Had to go in to hear faint music coming from inside.
The cave seemed to go on longer.
I came out into daylight. A park with a grassy bank, like the mirror image of the other.
Instead of the dead rosebush there was something green and blue that smelled nice. No butts.
Instead of the traffic there were people walking. The road was all grass and the crash barrier was like the altar rail at church.
Instead of going along the road, I went down to the corner of the park. There was a footpath and a fountain.

The streets were sort of familiar. Saw the warehouse with the big B6 on the side, except it didn't say that. It had two weird symbols on it. I went down toward Station Road but the street sign said something else.
A kid walked past me and laughed. I'm in my pajamas.
A woman, sort of dressed funny, came over to me and jabbered on in a foreign language. She was smiling and I guess she was being friendly.

She took my hand and we went back to the park. She waved me on into the cave again.
The music was still going, like temple gongs and birdsong.

When I came out it was night and the traffic was back and it was raining.

This morning I had mud on my feet and my PJs. Auntie V said the police had brought me home in the middle of the night. They found me sleepwalking.
I wish I could remember what happened.

Dream. Maybe.
Or am I remembering something I dreamt before?

The Singing. It's like a bass soloist, maybe a blues singer.
It echoes between the warehouses. It must be really loud 'cos it's a long way away off.
It makes me feel sad to listen to it. It's like you want it to stop but don't want it to end, kind of hopeless, kind of comforting.

I'm sitting on the marble railing. The sun is shining under the clouds and they're turning red. The breeze is warm. I'm really happy, just sitting and listening.

It's not a man's voice, maybe it's a buffalo's. A buffalo with the blues.
Such an enormous, beautiful sound.
I woke up in tears.

Okay, Theo, there it is.
Yesterday, I took a field trip to the park off the Edgware Road. It's just like I remember. Full of litter, empty cans, and the noise of traffic. It apparently haunted my dreams.

So, when I was younger, where the hell did I get the idea about the grassy walkway and the altar rail? – just as Uncle Teddy said – a marble balustrade.

He talked about the cave, the warehouses, and the streets. He even wrote about the damned plants in that stupid triangle of a bed.

So, go ahead, explain it to me.
He doesn't describe the messy park we know.
He describes the one I dreamt about.
How does one person write about something and another dream it?
How did he do that miles away and years before?

Curt

From: Theo03 < Theo5503@_________.us >

Subject: journal

Date: Mon, 08 Aug 2011

To: Bookman@_____________.co.uk

Thanks for sharing. Seriously.

I'm glad you remember that much. I'm surprised you don't know when the sleepwalking thing happened. I do.

The school nurse sent you to your Aunt's because you had something nasty and contagious and she didn't want you infecting the rest of us boarders.

It was the same month we were in the grip of Harrow's Alien Abduction Panic and JW got into all that trouble with his "reporting" about it in the student paper.

As for your memory of sitting on the marble balustrade – you know the answer. You've been there.

I know you have, because so have I. It isn't in Edgware.

Attached are the next two chapters. Uncle Teddy explains it better than I can.

Theo

Chapter Four

I wandered home, from park to park, on foot.

I spoke to no one save for one lone, and I suspected insane, photographer who claimed, amongst other things, to be documenting the return of the troops. I walked on as if with purpose, Allo carrying and pulling my bags behind me.

As we passed other Gre-tra, he occasionally exchanged a guttural snort or two. I overlooked the transgression and walked on in resolute silence.

I sent Allo first to the Mut-pel, my mother's right hand. I told him to say I was returning and wished to access my rooms before being announced.

He came back to me as I waited at the servants' door. All was well. I could use the service corridor and slip into my room without facing any questions.

I lay on my bed, my old bed, and stared at the ceiling. I listened to Allo unpack my bags.

"Sir?" he asked.

"What is it?"

"A place for this?"

He held the book of colorful photographs.

It seemed a strange thing, here in the familiar light of my room, a dirty object, an intrusion.

"I will take it now." I sat up and held out my hand.

"As you wish," he replied, almost, I thought, with a hint of a warning in his tone.

"No, not as I wish, but as I must."

I had the Mut-pel ask my mother to meet with me in one of her rooms. That was clue enough for Mother to know my return was not an easy one.

She sat in the large chair, her hands folded in her lap. I sat opposite, the book of colorful photographs clutched in mine.

"Welcome home, Son," she said, her voice carefully controlled, perhaps cautious until she knew what was happening.

"Thank you, Mother," I replied.

The Mut-pel stood at the periphery of her vision and Allo stood on the other side, just in my sight. Both seemed alert and fascinated.

"Mother, I return from service in the Chogren campaign. I bring back this object. It troubles me and I seek your advice."

She visibly relaxed. I could see her thinking with relief, *Oh, is that all!*

"Show me, please."

I handed her the book and sat back, waiting, ready for her to look through it for as long as she needed.

She took a while choosing her words. "In what way does this trouble you, Teh-di?"

I began slowly, trying to keep control of my emotions. "The Chogren are primitive. They lack the capacity to understand our language."

She nodded.

I continued, "Yet you hold in your hand the result of a technology of which we are not masters. They produce photographs showing natural colors."

"And they do it well," she agreed, perhaps missing my point, perhaps not.

"It troubles me that the Chogren may not be the primitives we thought them to be. If that is so, what do we say of Hal-fi's role in the campaign and his death at their hands? Of what do I say of their deaths at my hand?"

She nodded and again chose her words with the utmost care. "Teh-di, your concern for these strangers speaks of your good nature. I admire the way your heart reaches out to them. I do not deal in the intricacies of politics. You know this well; so, you came first to me and will go second to your father." She smiled a motherly smile. "You also know I cannot ease this trouble for you, much as my heart wishes it were within my power."

I did not reply. Perhaps I already had what I came for.

She continued, "These Chogren, perhaps even those pictured here, will find their proper place with us. Before, they were lost. Now, they are found. To be lost and not to try to find one's way, to be at a low—or even modest stage of achievement—and not seek improvement, are surely indications of a serious flaw. I do not think technology can help such weakness of character, do you? Consider if this is what is meant by 'primitive,' you may find your answer there."

Her words were a comfort.

"I will have to show this to Father. How best do you think I should...address the matter?"

She smiled again. "In the same way you have to me. I'm sure his answer will be the same—though much longer and more reasoned."

She stood and so did I. "Welcome home, Teh-di! We will celebrate tonight. Do not bring your worries to the table. Be at peace for the sake of your brothers and sisters. They will be pleased to see you."

"Thank you, Mother."

"Now, will your Gre-tra stay in the workers' lodgings?"

"Ah...No. He will remain with me for now."

Mother nodded and said to the Mut-pel, "Familiarize the Gre-tra with the ways of the household."

The Mut-pel replied, bowing, "Of course, Madam."

To Allo I said, "Be back to help me dress for dinner."

Allo nodded silently.

And so, I went across the gleaming hallway of the house alone to my father's offices.

"Teh-di! Why was I not told of your return? My boy! Your first tour of duty was a success, I understand. Welcome home!"

"Thank you, Father."

He looked into my eyes and I did not look away.

"What is it, Teh-di?"

"I return with a souvenir of Chogren. It has caused me some trouble of mind since I first looked inside it."

I handed the book across his desk. He took it and waved for me to sit down. He sat back in his chair and slowly, almost reverently, opened the cover to the first page.

"As you see..." I began.

He held up his hand for silence. I stopped. He turned the next page. I saw no change in his expression. He seemed thoughtful, a little amused, and appeared untroubled. When he had turned the last page he said quietly, "The Chogren women are pretty, are they not? Did you meet one of them?" He glanced up with a smile.

"No, Father. My trouble is not of that nature."

He nodded. "Good, good." He drew a deep breath and turned his face again from the book to mine. "Begin."

Most of the confidence I had built up dissolved.

"The Chogren are primitive. How can a primitive people have gone ahead of us in such technology?" My voice was betraying me, I sounded upset.

"Is that the basis of your proposition?"

I nodded. "I'm sorry; I could have phrased it more dispassionately."

"Indeed." He gave me a look from under his brow that I had seen at a hundred conversations around the dinner table, where he had trained us to speak clearly, logically, accurately, and we youngsters, far behind him in such skills, had so often failed to impress him.

He began his counterargument. "The technological issue is not a hard one. Our engineers will have such cameras as the Chogren build within a year. You did collect some I trust? And, no doubt, we will have gathered up individuals with the relevant expertise."

"I do not know, Father. I am not sure what such a device might look like having seen nothing during my tour resembling our cameras."

He nodded thoughtfully then continued, "But, if I hear the tone of what you say, I believe you wish to make a larger point. Perhaps you suspect that we have done the Chogren some degree of harm in bringing them—and their technological prowess—under our care?"

"You hold in your hand, Father, evidence against the claim that they are primitive. The colorful photographs and the technology behind them are relevant facts in the case."

"So, the case is proposed that the Chogren might not be primitive..." He glanced out of the window, the clouds were blushing with the lowering sun. "Interesting."

I waited while he thought.

"Let us take the evidence for the claim..." he began again, "They lack the capacity to speak our language. Is this not so?"

"I saw none alive long enough to hear one try. Yet there were diplomatic missions, I thought. Was that not how hostilities began?"

Father thought for while. "I believe no verbal communication was possible. We attempted dialogue and were met with violence."

"Then that evidence is not certain," I replied. "We cannot know if a lack of communication was due to inability or...unwillingness."

"Then let us build our claim rather on their unwillingness. Violence is the common lot of the primitive. To react to that which you do not understand with aggression is the mark of a lesser mind. Is this not so?"

"Yet violence itself, while within the realm of the primitive, is not limited to the primitive, is it? There are other reasons to take up arms than the one suggested. One cannot be sure that aggression came from fear in this case."

He frowned. "Where else would it originate?"

"Perhaps in an assessment of our unknown intent or perhaps of our unknown might. The Chogren may have, using a more sophisticated analysis than we have heretofore credited them with, made a judgment that they could defeat us."

He laughed lightly. "I think you move the Chogren from the primitive to the stupid! A modest win that, perhaps, I may grant you..."

"Father, perhaps they are like us?"

At this he did not laugh or even smile. He moved the closed book back across the desk.

"It is we who have the empire. That is a fact relevant in this case. They have no empire—also a fact relevant in this case. Why has such a state of affairs come about? If they were like us, perhaps they would be us, and we them. No, Teh-di, you argue a specific case and think it speaks against a general truth! There are no other peoples 'like us,' nor can there be. The only matter in dispute is whether the Chogren are less primitive than our other neighbors."

I heard his words, but in my mind, and I think in his, was the presence of my brother, his lost son, the young general who oversaw the beginning of our war against the Chogren.

"Indeed, as to the specific example you bring, I can tell you that one engineering fluke does not make as big a difference as you think," he said. "I have seen technologies arise for a limited local application that would have remained unknown if we had not introduced them across the span of our commonwealth."

His voice was not that of the calm debater but of a man holding back great feeling. He recovered himself in a short silence.

"I will share something with you, Son, that I want you always to remember." He did not smile, but the informality of his tone moved me. "We are unique. But our skills are of a particular nature. We are very good at Empire—a skill that overarches all others, for we can acquire all that we need thereby. Our system of supervisors is so well-developed that people of all kinds have been seamlessly folded into our city, into our service, and remain there. Yes, the supervisors may, by nature of their profession, have to be extremely tough at times, but how different these people all are, how different their skills and capacities! Yet all of them, we welcome, we absorb. This is our particular skill, our unique technology, if you will, to be able to draw people into our life, to share our greatness with them, to rescue them from the squalor of their own poor lives and give them a place with us."

He was silent. In my mind's eye I saw the faces of the Chogren family looking out from their photographs, and I knew they too would disagree, for as we give them a place, we are doing it by force of arms and without consent. I knew, at least in the case of the Chogren, we had rescued them from a life more technologically adept than our own. We had, as far as I could remember, never stopped to consider whether their poor lives might have in any way been better than ours.

My father relaxed in his chair. "I hope we have set your mind to rest! Do not think that you are the first soldier to come home having been exposed to a wider reality and found himself doubting his place. Doubt no more. Put this book on your shelf and do not worry about it again.

"I am glad you are back. Put aside your troubles. You have duties to perform, as do we all. Not always as we wish, but as we must."

He was dismissing me. I knew there more arguments to bring, and the matter was far from settled, but his tone was clear. I left the room certain for the first time in my life that I, a loosely constructed young man, was right and my father, the central supporting column of my life, was wrong.

***

Dinner was a disaster. I said little more than the pleasantries required. My youngest sister, Pul-no, was nervous of me, as she had been of each of her brothers upon his return from service. When she dropped her knife onto an empty plate, the noise was like an explosion and breaking glass. I was up from my seat and heading to rescue my fallen men, my chair foolishly hitting the floor behind me. Pul-no was in tears, Mother was annoyed, and Father silent. Humiliated, I retreated, with a piece of bread in my hand, back to my room.

Allo was there. There was something odd about him. That perhaps would be an understatement at normal times, but this night his manner was especially so.

"Allo? Is something wrong?"

He walked away from me, and back, then looked up directly into my eyes—a rare event.

"Sir. Your brother...who died. His Gre-tra. Still here. Here in this house."

I thought for a moment. I didn't remember ever seeing my Hal-fi's Gre-tra, though I assumed he had had one.

"My mother probably took him in. It is sometimes done...in such circumstances."

Allo nodded. "He is old. He is old."

"Can he no longer work? Is that the problem?"

Allo nodded again. "Old. Tired."

"What can be done for him?"

Allo walked away and back again, in what for a Gre-tra must be great agitation.

"Food. Rest. Less work. Other duties?"

I was impressed by his eloquence. I had rarely heard him speak so much in one breath.

"You are concerned for him. That speaks well of you."

"Old. Old are...respected, yes?"

"Always." The word came out of my mouth with a vigor that surprised me.

He looked at me and waited. It was clear he wanted me to do something.

I sighed. "For whom does he provide service?"

"Sir?"

"Which member of the family does he do work for?"

Allo shook his head. "Mut-pel. Mut-pel beats him. Mut-pel throws food. Scraps. Mut-pel, not good."

I sighed again and stood looking out of the window at the path tracing through the dark of the lawn. "I don't have time to sort out my mother's domestic problems, Allo. Perhaps tomorrow I can ask her to check..."

Allo interrupted me—a true indication of his distress. "Sir! Old!

Onvi is old. Respected. Must help!"

I turned and shouted, "Very well! Bring him to me! Let's get this out of the way!"

Allo ran from the room.

I could not tell that Onvi was old. He appeared like any Gre-tra. Perhaps his movements were a little slower than Allo's, but that could indicate insolence or ill will just as easily.

I sat on my bed and Allo and Onvi stood side by side before me.

"You may speak freely with me, Gre-tra. Your name is Onvi?" I began.

"Onvi, Sir. I was Gre-tra to your late brother. He was a great man, a man of conscience and deliberation. He was kind to me and I miss him."

I was stunned. Here was a Gre-tra in full command of himself and speaking like an Aleronden. His speech had a foreign cadence, but the words were clear and grammatical.

"How in the name of all things holy, do you come to speak with such skill?"

Onvi bowed. "I am old, Sir. I have listened for many years to the words of my masters. Your late brother encouraged me. He spoke to me often. That I can express my thoughts to you is a gift I received from him. And I thank you for allowing me to speak with you."

"No wonder the Mut-pel doesn't like you! You have crossed a line by taking such a task of learning upon yourself. But if Hal-fi encouraged you, perhaps I should not go against him. Can you read also?"

Onvi nodded. "Certain things I am able to read, yes, Sir."

"Unbelievable! What were you thinking, Hal-fi? Why did you place such a burden on a Gre-tra?"

Onvi made no answer but stood and waited for me, as he should. But now it was different. Even Allo was different. It was clear they both understood the dynamics of the situation. I was inheriting a problem of my brother's making. What was it Mother had said about my "good nature?"

If the two Gre-tra had understood how close I came to killing them both, there in my room, they would not have waited so patiently for my reaction. I still had my service weapon and my instinct was to use it to teach these workers not to overreach their place.

I was sitting on my bed. Next to me was the book of colorful photographs. In front of me was a Gre-tra who could speak its thoughts in our language. Two physical indications that the diagnosis of "primitive" was less clear than I had been taught. It underpinned so much of our society and its dealings with others. I was still troubled by my interview with Father. I was still burning inside from my lack of decorum at dinner. Blowing the heads off these two would have been such a great relief. I would have enjoyed it.

It sobers me now, as I write, to think how the course of so many lives pivoted on such a moment.

Instead I said quietly, "Onvi, do not reveal...your gift...to anyone else in this house. Advice, I'm sure, my brother also gave you. I will take you into my service while I work out what to do with you. No, Allo, as well as you, not instead."

"Sir?" Allo looked alarmed.

"I will have two Gre-tra. I do not care how it looks to the family."

Allo nodded, relieved.

Onvi bowed low and said, "My life is in your hands, Sir."

I stood and said, "Yes, it is. Remember that. I will protect you not out of regard for you, but for my brother. Abuse your position at your peril! Do you understand that?"

"I do, Sir."

Allo was looking alarmed again. Onvi said, "Excuse me, Sir." He turned to Allo and made several noises in his direction. Allo nodded and they both turned and bowed to me again.

"Wait here," I ordered and left my room. I found my mother crossing the hall.

"Mother?"

"Teh-di? Are you feeling better?"

"Thank you, Mother, I am quite well. I have received a report that your Mut-pel has been abusing a worker under her command."

She smiled, "Your time in service has changed your manner, hasn't it, Teh-di?"

I wasn't sure what she meant. "I wish to take Hal-fi's Gre-tra."

"Really? Why? He's rather old, they tell me."

"I have use for him."

"What will you do with the other one?"

I shrugged. "Keep him."

"Two Gre-tra? People will think you injured or incapacitated."

"So be it. Will you tell the Mut-pel or shall I?"

"I'm going to bed. You can tell her I agreed. But really Teh-di, you should have a care what people will say."

"Yes, Mother. Good night."

I found the Mut-pel working in the kitchen. I threw her against the wall and holding her by the throat said, "Treat those under your command with respect. If I hear of any cruelty on your part again I will not consult with Mother first, I will come straight here and kill you. My brother's Gre-tra is mine and under my protection." I stared into her terrified eyes. "Continue with your work."

I left the Mut-pel gasping on the floor.

Chapter Five

Onvi snored. But I would not have slept anyway.

I was up early and sent orders out for certain equipment to be delivered to the house. I then made an appointment with Father.

When the hour came I went, with my two Gre-tra at my side, into his office.

"Teh-di? Why are they here?" was his greeting.

"I will not go anywhere without them, Father. They are my assistants." Before he could express his shock at my words, I continued.

"Father, I wish you to apply for a year's postponement of my next deployment. One year, exactly. I will spend the time photographing The Great Parks and writing a book about their architectures and histories. It will be the definitive book on the subject."

"A photographic book?" He was about to laugh.

"Yes, with photographs as we know them, white and gray and black. I need to finish the book before the cameras capable of producing colorful images are available. As soon as they are, I will send my assistants out once more to reproduce each photograph in that manner. I will then publish a colorful version of my book with no extra work on my part. I shall see twice the revenue for once the work. And...I will be positioned ahead of the market. It will be The First Great Colorful Book."

He laughed, but not with the ridicule I assumed he had been preparing. He seemed to see the business sense in what I said.

"Teh-di...Teh-di...You surprise me! Yesterday you were a soldier with a troubled mind. Today you are a businessman with a keen eye. I'm impressed!"

"Thank you, Father. But my success hinges on the deferment. Timing will be critical."

He nodded; the case was argued successfully. He asked, "And why the...assistants?"

"I have ordered the best available camera and equipment. I imagine it will be heavy. I doubt one back will be able to carry it so far."

He nodded again. "So be it! Your mother will be relieved." He returned to the papers on his desk and the appointment was over.

Once back in my room Onvi said, "Sir? I did not understand all that was said in your father's office."

"No, that's all right. I won an argument with him. That was the point of the matter. It was the first battle in my new campaign. For you, it will mean fresh air, walks in the parks, and history lessons in The Greatness that is Aleronde. For me, it means time to think...walks in the parks, and a chance to improve my photographic skills."

"And there was mention made of something heavier than one back can carry?"

I was impressed; he really missed nothing.

I nodded. "There is equipment arriving tomorrow. We will strip it down to its barest essentials. There will be not a thread of weight we do not need. But we will need a little private money. My military pay may be long in coming, I fear, and Mother has first call on it all the while I sleep and eat here."

I went to my bag of personal effects. Drawing out several wrapped parcels, I sat on the floor with the Gre-tra and laid out my share of the Chogren spoils.

"We will go to The Park of Peace first. There will be people there who will pay cash for items such as these. We will take one sample of everything and see how much each is worth. Keep alert for those who have seen these things before. We need fresh buyers who can be persuaded they are more valuable than they actually are."

Allo was looking from my face to Onvi's and back again.

I waved my hand and said, "Tell him!"

Onvi made noises at Allo. It took a while. Allo seemed to disagree with parts of the plan.

Onvi eventually said, "Perhaps, Sir, The Park of Peace would not be entirely safe for such transactions as you propose. Allo has rightly suggested that The Park of Music may serve us better. While good citizens such as yourself, Sir, are enraptured by the performances, servants and the staff of the park have time on their hands and much quiet and invisible work is accomplished."

I laughed out loud. "Really?" I shook my head. "And you have seen all this?"

Onvi bowed his head a little, averting his eyes. "I have spent much time in military service, Sir. Allo's recent work was also within the confines of the ships. However, when our masters return for leave or are brought back to heal, we have had...opportunities to come to know this."

"Again I learn about how my city works...Good. The Park of Music it is. There is a concert there tomorrow night. The family will go. We will go and take photographs."

"Sir?"

"We will stay at the edges and not sit with the others. No one will notice us once the music begins."

Onvi nodded.

I smiled. "And then you can introduce me to this part of my world that I have never seen."

***

Over the months that followed we became something of an

institution, The Photographer and his Two Gre-tra. My sisters were flattered by the attention it brought them at school. My mother continued to be puzzled.

Onvi and Allo had unguessed business acumen. I soon trusted them enough to work contacts on their own without my presence. The Chogren souvenirs were soon exhausted, replaced by other items traded and bartered with other Gre-tra in shadowy huddles at the corners of gatherings, under the shade of bridges, and even in range of the unhearing ears of my fellow Aleronden citizens, who took their haggling for sounds without meaning.

I would not become rich thusly, but it covered photographic supplies, traveling costs, and some entertainment. It was enough for the project to continue apace. I was writing in the evenings and gathering notes made in earlier years, revisiting long forgotten classes from school. The Book of The Great Parks was taking shape.

I chose my battles with Father carefully. When he ordered my presence at certain functions, I gritted my teeth and attended, arriving only just in time and leaving as soon as was seemly. Happily, only a few times people made loud noises or sudden moves that set off another vivid memory of violence. When I could, I used The Book as The Great Excuse.

I persuaded him to give me two rooms at the end of the wing where he had his offices. They were seldom used and one had the supreme advantage of its own door to the passage at the side of the house, which led to a private gate. Once installed there, we three conspirators could come and go at will without deference to the family or the household routines. The second room we fitted out as our darkroom.

I was happy, in as much as a man can be, knowing he is alone in the world, alone in his conclusions about the empire he serves, alone in his reactions to anything that might remind him of battle and his fallen men. No, I was not happy in the ordinary sense; I was resolved, and for a time, that would suffice.

And then, unseen in its coming, unlooked-for in its consequences, was my return to Revelsar and the Manam Paravel.

I was documenting the Manam Way. I decided only one image of it should be included in the book, but it had to represent the many grassy miles of the Way. I was looking for something else beside the endless balustrade, the cropped grass, and blue and green tiles of roofs below.

I stopped and sat for a while, watching people stroll along the grass, listening to the sounds of the city around me, and looking at clouds high up and moving fast.

"Allo, I have something to show you," I said, "This came today."

I took from my bag an envelope containing a photograph. It had been sent by the photographer who had stopped us shortly after we disembarked from our ship. I had not expected to hear from him again, but he had kept his word and sent a copy of the image he had taken that day.

Allo's reaction surprised me. Perhaps he had never seen a photograph of himself before, perhaps he saw something I could not see. He let out a small sigh and reached a finger to the image and drew around the shape of his own face.

Onvi watched in enigmatic silence. Allo looked up at me, withdrew his hand and said nothing.

I asked him, "Is what we are doing better than being in the war?"

He looked at the ground and said, "You come back. Not die in battle."

I nodded. "I'll take that as a 'yes.'"

We walked too far that day. It was warm in the streets, but cooler on the Way. I found it easier to keep walking there than think of descending and hiring transport home. That is the singular magic of the Manam Way.

Late, too late, I paused to consider a vista of long brown roofs—the warehouses of Revelsar! I saw the large numbers that adorn the corners of each building. I felt an excitement rise in me that I did not understand.

We eventually descended into streets of housing, the homes of lower-class Alerondens who are the supervisors, the citizen captains to the armies of workers who operated the warehouses and the many small factories to the north.

As we walked, I remembered that these houses had looked bigger in my youth, the streets had seemed cleaner, the area had held more glamour.

We came to a sign indicating the Manam Paravel. Onvi became excited. Allo, it seemed to me, was trying to calm him, as if he did not want me to see his elder's emotion.

I had been in their company now for several months with no more than a few hours absence. I had a growing instinct for what passed between them. I said nothing and let them debate.

We walked a short way and I heard a noise. It was a noise that I had heard before, many times, but without knowing what made it. It was a low rumble. A rumble with an edge of music to it.

Around the corner, we came upon the source.

Inside the open freight doors of a warehouse, a series of chains rose in the air. They closed around the wrists of a creature ten, perhaps twelve, feet tall. As we stood and wondered at its size, I marveled at the blue hue to its skin and its huge eyes, shaped like those of a Gre-tra. It was dressed in a ragged jacket and rough cloth leggings. It stood upon bare feet, huge and misshapen, with claws large enough to disembowel a man.

It strained against its chains, stood tall, lifted its head, and sang. Such a deep sadness rushed upon us. The ground shook. The air trembled. We were rooted in our place as the melody swept under and around us. Such beauty, such feeling! I was sure it knew what it was singing. This was no ignorant beast, though employed as a beast of burden in the warehouse. Its song was the very spirit of loss and desolation. Night watchmen came with sticks and pushed the beast back from the doors. They closed the shutters, cutting down the volume, but the song continued.

Into this music-filled air came the smell of frying. We listened as long as we could but the smell eventually won us over; it was irresistible.

"Come!" I said, "Let's see what they eat here."

We found a small area of grass, untended and worn, at the junction of three roads. The wrought fences that had once surrounded the grass lay flattened on the ground, half-buried. Upon the remains of the grass were several carts, billowing smoke, steam, and exotic smells.

I surveyed the proprietors; several wore dirty uniforms. Their hair was unwashed, their faces grimy with soot from cooking. I knew them and their story at once—I feared it had almost been mine. They would have had a tour of duty in the colonies, experiences enough to challenge all sanity, and an abrupt return to a life both dissonant and uncomfortable. After a time of dislocation they would have begun again, working where they could, living from day to day, unhelped and forgotten.

The one cart not so manned was run by a stooped, round-shouldered creature with his head on his chest. I knew his kind, and I knew the smell of what he sold.

I had a plate of fragrant custard in my hand in the twinkling of an eye. As I ate with unbridled relish, my assistants appeared to come to a resolution of the matter that had so preoccupied Onvi.

"Do you eat this?" I asked them.

They shook their heads and pointed at the next cart. Onvi said, "This, though, we remember."

A former soldier leaned over his cart and looked me up and down. "Officer?"

I nodded. "Back from First Tour. I'm photographing the parks."

The soldier laughed, perhaps at the thought of something better than another tour, perhaps at my idiocy. "What will you take? Marsu? Pol? Tregg with brown or green sauce?"

I looked at the Gre-tra. "Your choice. I have what I need."

Onvi addressed the soldier and said, "Does he make the Pol?" He indicated the Gre-tra behind the cart, working the steaming pots.

The soldier raised an eyebrow at being questioned by a servant and glanced at me before replying. "He does. Best I ever tasted."

"Pol, please," Onvi said to me, his eyes on the floor.

"Pol, please," said Allo, adding "Four portions."

Onvi gasped at his forwardness. I laughed. The soldier laughed and shook his head. "I like a customer who knows what he wants!"

Four portions of Pol were laid out on the camera bag. I sat near one end with my spice dish, the Gre-tra at the other. They addressed each plate in turn, both taking from the same one, in a kind of communion.

We had worked out a system of signals for our business negotiations, a way Onvi could warn me of dangers or duplicity.

As they ate, he made three signs to me.

Firstly, he signed to me that the Gre-tra at this cart was one we should speak to.

Secondly, he indicated that we were in the wrong place.

The third sign I was not expecting. He believed there was something of exceptional value to be had.

With such a set of signals that seemed contradictory, I was unsure of the next step. I knew he would not speak out for fear of being overheard. This was a game in which I would have to watch and let him take the lead. I had seen enough during our other adventures to allow it and not worry unduly about the consequences.

The food done, Onvi signaled again that this was the wrong place. He spoke to Allo, who muttered and looked annoyed.

I stood and stretched. Onvi fussed over picking up the used plates. I looked to the soldier at the cart and said, "Thank you and good night!"

He nodded.

Allo had taken up the bag and was dragging the satchel that Onvi carried. I picked up the tripod. Onvi was over by the cart throwing the plates onto a pile of similar trash. Allo set off and Onvi did not follow. I hesitated, but Onvi disappeared behind the cart.

I followed Allo across the street, down a turn to the right, and suddenly we were in the Manam Paravel.

The clouds overhead were pink with the setting sun. The park glowed with a warm light. The marble balustrade at the edge of the Manam Way was a sharp silhouette.

"Quick, Allo! The camera!" I shouted.

We assembled the camera in a great hurry. I used the one long-exposure plate I carried and the light held for me. I knew it would be a good one. I could imagine it as the cover image for the book. It would be more than an image of a piece of architecture; it would be an iconic symbol of Aleronde capturing the mystery, the stability and order, the grace.

I was aglow with spice, clean air, and the joy of being in the right place at the right time. For the first time in many months, all was well.

As we disassembled the gear, Onvi returned to help us. There were still citizens strolling in the park; we talked softly.

"Find something?" I asked him.

"I heard news, gossip, strange tales, Sir."

"Anything of interest to buy or sell?"

Onvi paused in tying up the bag to look briefly into my eyes. "What price has knowledge, Sir?"

"Are we to stay here the night? Or shall we return another day?"

Onvi did not reply. Allo was muttering again.

"You need to see your contact again?" I pressed.

Onvi shook his head and said, "No, Sir. I do not wish to mislead you. There is no treasure here. There is a mystery here."

"Oh, why do I feel this will take a while?"

"Long stories are worth the listening, Sir."

"Some are."

I took them up to the Way, and we sat with our backs against the low marble edge, looking down into the Manam Paravel. The few late strollers were heading away in the gathering twilight.

"Have you been here before, Sir?"

"Many times. I played here as a child. My first school stands on the other side of the Way."

Onvi nodded. Allo muttered.

"Is he all right?" I asked.

"He thinks me old and foolish, Sir."

"Well, he must be at least half right."

Onvi nodded again. "There are stories, Sir, about this place. Wild people are seen here. People who speak languages we do not know. They appear at night sometimes. Sometimes in the day. Do you know the cave, Sir?"

"I do. I was there. I have been in the far chamber, where only the small and thin can go."

"Sometimes, we hear, people go in and do not return."

Allo got up and walked a few steps away and back again. "Sir! Do not listen. Old tales. Mad tales."

"You don't believe him either, Allo?"

Onvi answered, "He objects *because* he believes."

I was beginning to be interested. "Explain."

Onvi sighed. "Allo's father came out from that cave, Sir. I knew him while he lived."

"What do you mean he 'came out from that cave'?"

"One day his business took him into such a cave far from here and yet he walked out from it here in this park. He was caught by supervisors and sent into military service. He knew nothing of Aleronde. He knew nothing of service. It was hard for him."

Allo muttered, "Mad stories."

"Onvi, it is getting dark, we're tired. Get to the point. Where does this become valuable?"

Onvi shook his head. "If it were possible, what would it not be worth? If here is a truth not known?"

I sighed. "That sort of value is hard to count, isn't it? What do you suggest? We send customers into the cave in the hope they disappear? That we set up a cart and sell food to visitors from the other side? How long would we wait before we saw such a thing, Onvi?"

"I do not know, Sir. But the Gre-tra I spoke with has seen both things. He knows of several visitors who live here still. He has seen a fellow Gre-tra go in and not come back."

"And you believe him? Is he not just telling tales for amusement?"

Onvi looked up with his black eyes and said sadly, "I do not know the words to make you understand, Sir. I know it to be true. He does not lie."

I shook my head. "One may be sure and yet also mistaken. Such things do not happen. Many wonders are real. Look, how far did we travel in the ship? We walked in the land of the Chogren! How marvelous is that? But it is a marvel of engineering, not of magic."

"Magic, Sir? I do not say so. There are many things that people will try to achieve if they have need. Perhaps what happens here is the result of someone's work? Do the Chogren understand your ship and how it travels? Perhaps it seems magic to them?"

I laughed. "I feel I am arguing like my father. To make a doorway from somewhere else into this cave is a preposterous thing to do! Who would want to come here, to this park? Someone of questionable sanity perhaps? I can think of much better places to go, can't you?"

"No, Sir. I cannot."

I was brought up short by his answer. He was both serious and certain.

"Go on."

"One more, one less would not draw attention here. One may come and go to the main routes unnoticed. This is a good place for such a thing. Especially if it were some natural force someone wanted to conduct experiments on. Here, no one would see."

I nodded. "You win the case, Onvi. I am convinced. Though I am convinced of something that cannot be."

Onvi hesitated, then spoke. “Perhaps, Sir, we could go inside and see?”

In the silence Allo got up and stepped away, and back, in a small circle.

“You wish me to go into the cave at night? Do I not have enough of a strange reputation already for going around with the two of you? Now you wish to add this?”

“Look there!” Onvi was pointing down the bank and toward where the cave mouth should have been hidden in shadow. A glow came from inside the cave; its entrance clearly outlined, and silhouetted against the glow was the shape of a Gre-tra.

“What is that?” I muttered—to myself, for Onvi and Allo were already down the bank and running faster than I had ever seen them move. They were in the cave before I was halfway across the grass. I heard their voices echoing back from the rock.

As I followed them in, lights flashed. Ahead of me, in the eerie glow, I saw Onvi and Allo standing, looking back. Onvi held up his hand in a sign meaning “stay back.” It seemed to me that Allo signed “too late.”

Behind them stood the Gre-tra I had seen silhouetted against the cave mouth. He wore a fine uniform and held up a device the like of which I had never seen. The light faded and I heard pleasing music that was high toned but without rhythm. I felt my way inward, along the smooth wall, left, right, and left again.

I stumbled into a sunny day. A dead bush caught my bag, and I staggered and fell. A pale blue sky flecked with white clouds stretched over the park. I pushed myself up and stared. I was still in the park, the triangular park, its shape had not altered, but a roar of vehicles sounded from the Manam Way, the smell of fuel was in the air. The grass was not cared for.

Onvi and Allo were nowhere to be seen. Instead were several people in strange clothes staring at me.

"You!" I called, "Tell me. Where are the three Gre-tra gone?"

The nearest woman frowned and shook her head. A small crowd gathered around me. None could understand my questions. I ran back into the cave, but found no exit.

Soon, uniformed men came and helped me into a vehicle. One laughed much but could say nothing I could recognize as words. I was bewildered. Where was this? And how had this been accomplished?

Somehow I had been tricked by my servants.

From: Bookman@_____________.co.uk

Subject: Current Project

Date: Wed, 10 Aug 2011

To: Theo03 < Theo5503@_________.us >

Not so fast.

The park IS in Edgware. I was just there.

The marble-edged grass walk was in a dream. I haven't been there.

Do you mean you dreamt it too?

It looks to me like you're putting words in your uncle's mouth.

Enough of this. Time to tell me what you're up to.

Talk to me.

Curt

From: Theo04 < Theo2204@_________.tv >

Subject: Last Chapter

Date: Wed, 10 Aug 2011

To: Bookman@_____________.co.uk

Don't give me that "it was a dream" nonsense. You know damn well it wasn't.

I'll admit I was willing to discount the whole thing too. Then I started to read Teddy's descriptions of places I've been – places you've been too. My experience was similar to yours. I just didn't know what to make of it until I opened Marjory's trunk and found the memoir.

I wanted to get you to the point you'd remember it all. I know you. I trust you to be honest and see the truth of it.

We've both been in Aleronde. Teddy wasn't insane, though he should have been considering what happened to him.

You asked me if this was fact or fiction. You've now worked out for yourself which it is.

Attached are the last chapter and a photo Uncle Teddy had tucked in with the manuscript.

Theo

Chapter Six

My first days were dark.

Then I awoke one morning realizing that those around me, though they had had ample opportunity and I had given them good cause, had done me no harm.

The opposite was true; they had done me nothing but good. They had given me food (of a sort), shelter, facilities for washing and sleeping. In fact, although without a servant, I lived more comfortably than aboard the ship traveling forth and back from Chogren.

When I had tried to escape from the hospital, they had used no more force than required to prevent me.

They had tried to communicate with me, and I with them, to our mutual frustration. Many people came and made noises to me trying, I suppose, to find a common tongue.

But that morning, I realized I was in no actual danger from these strangers and began to see where I was and what I was.

I was the primitive. To them, I lacked the capacity to speak their language. I had reacted with unpredictable violence. I now sat in wonder seeing new technology and strange techniques, as if I were observing magicians.

They were the masters, and I the overwhelmed.

My healing began with a pen and a pad of paper. I disappointed my doctor by producing page after page of Aleronden script which he could not decipher nor I explain. But he was pleased perhaps that I was attempting to express myself in ways other than violence.

I wrote much about Allo and Onvi and their incredible betrayal. I wrote long and detailed postulations on the cave and who was responsible for its apparent capabilities. Who were the intelligent Gre-tra, somewhere beyond the empire, who wore uniforms and could produce a mechanism of such wonder? If it allowed them passage to one place while sending me to another, how many other places might it encompass? Do all its entrances look like the Manam Paravel?

To this day, though, I cannot understand why they would make such a path between this world and Aleronde, nor why they should make its appearance and operation so infrequent as if a matter of random chance.

I wondered if Onvi had planned long. Had the vendor's Gre-tra been but one of a series of conspirators? I wondered at the meaning of their final signs to me. Was Onvi's warning not to follow because he knew what would happen to me and wished me to avoid this fate? Was Allo laughing as he told me I was too late to save myself?

Happily, those in attendance around me could read nothing of the vitriol I included in my scribblings.

I wrote also about the men who died under my command, about my brother, Hal-fi, about the Chogren. Day by day, the pages piled higher, and my pain began to ease.

Eventually, I began to write more kindly of the Gre-tra. From my lonely vantage point, I recognized the first glimmer of empathy; I realized at one point that I felt sorry for Allo's father, whose name I had never heard spoken. I wondered at the relationships between the Gre-tra: connections unguessed at by us their masters and loves, inspirations, and influences about which we neither knew nor cared. Who was the Gre-tra my father and I had watched gunned down before our house that warm summer night?

I grew to accept my new role, being at the mercy of strange creatures. They looked like me—they would have been able to pass unnoticed along the byways of Aleronde—and yet they were not like me. They seemed intent on my succor. They gave me orders and limited my movements, but required of me no work. They were content, enthusiastic sometimes, as I learned my first few words of English, and patient when I tried to share something of my past.

It stands as a testimony to them and to the conditions into which I was rescued, that one of the first English words I learned was "trauma." I grew to understand they believed something catastrophic had happened to me. They were both correct and mistaken.

***

And so you see me, an Aleronden officer, son to a famous family, in a mental hospital, brought low to the point of being overturned. I was held in the position of the empire's enemies, unable to comprehend or resist the sudden change that had exploded around me.

And yet my transformation was not complete; I yet had further to fall.

Another morning, pen in my hand, piles of papers at my elbow, a young woman came into my room to interview me. Thus is a young man truly brought low. Marjory was her name, and soon I was in love.

Under her gentle tutelage, I came to speak more and more English. I still wrote in my own script and dreamed in my own tongue, but eventually that also changed.

If I have one complaint of her, it is that she has never pronounced my name with the correct emphasis, and so I am forever Teddy.

Against me I know she has many complaints, the foremost of which is my urge to cook each exotic spice into my custard. Perhaps, one day, I will discover what I'm looking for.

With her support, I was released. Finally I had the chance to see and explore this new world. My dreams of strange forests came true with Marjory at my side.

I went often to the park and to the cave. Never have I seen it glow or heard its music. I have found nothing there but a chamber with an opening too narrow for an adult to access—just as I knew it before. I go there rarely now. My disappointment at what I fail to find seems an insult to my wife and my new friends. Would I return through it to Aleronde if I could? Please, do not ask me.

For I worried then, as I still worry now, for Aleronde. I have seen with my own eyes a Gre-tra in uniform using a technology beyond ours-of such a different order as to make the color cameras of the Chogren seem a small matter. If the Gre-tra, those simplest and most pliant of people, could perform such a technological miracle as transportation across the distances without ships, then Aleronde is doomed.

Why do I write "if"? I sit writing in an alien chair through that miracle. Aleronde is doomed.

For we have made our world by piecing it together with those whom we have gathered. We have, rightly or wrongly, in the name of ennobling them, included them in our empire. We have placed them in our houses and factories. They, and all the others, are everywhere. If they should conspire to attack us, to undo what we have done, what defense would we have? They have a secret entrance to our city, at what point will they begin to use it? Our supervisors are few; they are many.

Our security is built in part on the assumption of our superiority. I fear my family and my friends in Aleronde know little of how weak that pillar has become. The Chogren could have told us. The Gre-tra may yet. What other peoples have we misunderstood? What may that misunderstanding yet cost?

As I grow older, I accept that such a battle, if a battle it becomes, is not mine to fight. I wonder about the girl from Garton.

Did she bear a child from me? Does he wear a uniform? Of my Aleronden nephews and nieces, what hopes have they of bright days and peaceful nights?

My home, my youth, my love are Aleronde. Aleronde The Great! Aleronde The Feared! Aleronde The Magnificent!

I dream of that place.

Photograph

Email CB 10Aug2011

From: Bookman@_____________.co.uk

Subject: Re: Last Chapter

Date: Wed, 10 Aug 2011

To: Theo04 < Theo2204@_________.tv >

Theo, you are a bastard and a lying one. Before I buy you your usual pint, I am going to punch you fair and square in the face and knock you onto your bony posterior.

You sent me this manuscript – and asked me not show it to anyone else – just to try and get me to remember something??

What kind of an idiot are you?

So, congratulations.

Now what?

At least when it was a dream, I had an explanation.

Teddy isn't in a position to explain how the cave worked. Aleronde sounds like nowhere I'd want to go even if, as he predicted, it's not already burnt to the ground.

Theo, I'm a publisher. What the hell do you want from me? What do you want me to do with Uncle Teddy and his damned memoir?

Your former friend,

Curt

From: Theo04 < Theo2204@_________.tv >

Subject: Re: Last Chapter

Date: Wed, 10 Aug 2011

To: Bookman@_____________.co.uk

My dearest Curtis,

I admit I owe you at least a pint of good beer.

What to do with Uncle Teddy's memoir?

Like you said, you're a publisher: PUBLISH THE BOOK!

I've attached other letters from Marjory to Doris.

I feel for Marjory, especially because of what she discovered. How awful!

She died about seven years after these last two letters.

I don't want to let her down. I don't want to let Uncle Teddy down. I believe a responsibility has been placed on you and me.

At the very least, I want to study the cave.

Theo

The Chimes

Upper Malbury

31 August 1979

Dear Sis,

It's almost a year since Teddy left us. I was reading through his papers again.

Oh, Sis, I've been to Teddy's cave.

You remember how he used to sneak off in the early days and visit that park by the Edgware Road? I took him there once. I can't remember if you and Rob were ever there.

It seemed so important to him. I suppose I was hoping paying it a visit might somehow keep him a bit closer.

I sat on a bench in the park opposite the cave reading some of Teddy's writings. I looked up at one point; the park was empty and quiet. When the sun goes round behind the rocks, the cave is really just a dark shadow.

There was light and a noise from the cave. As I watched, a dwarf came out – it was wearing a hood so I didn't see the face, but I'm sure it was just the sort Teddy used to describe. He put down some sort of machine – like a big radio or an old-style record player.

After he went back into the cave, the light went out. I was hoping it wasn't a bomb, and wondering whom to call, when the light and noise came back, the dwarf trotted out, picked up his machine, and disappeared inside again.

I was awake the whole time. It wasn't a dream.

I've never felt so wretched in my life. He was telling the truth, Sis! Teddy's fantasy wasn't a fantasy. I tried for eighteen years to persuade him. I never believed him, and now it's too late. I don't know what to do.

Love,

M.

The Chimes
Upper Malbury
16 September 1979

Dear Sis,

Thanks. I do feel a bit better now. But I miss him so.

Let's agree not to talk about it anymore. There's nothing we can do. Maybe we can leave Teddy's book to the younger folk and see what they make of it.

Speaking of whom, that Theo is so adorable, riding on the back of young Bob's enormous hound!

I know Rob's legs are playing up, but try and come for Christmas.

Love,

M.

From: Bookman@_____________.co.uk

Subject: Re: Last Chapter

Date: Wed, 10 Aug 2011

To: Theo04 <Theo2204@_________.tv>

Let's be clear.

I feel no responsibility to members of your family. Why would you think I do? I run a business, that's the end of this story.

Are you seriously considering studying the cave to try and go through it? To do what?

And publish this? Who would believe it?

Curt

From: Theo05 < Theo4505@_________.tv >

Subject: The Problem

Date: Thu, 11 Aug 2011

To: Bookman@_____________.co.uk

Dear Curt,

You believe it.

Besides, it's true. That's enough of a reason to publish, isn't it?

Here are some more reasons.

Teddy saw the Gre-tra working the cave. He never figured out how or when they might do it again. Onvi thought it was some kind of natural phenomenon they were exerting control over. The Gre-tra seem passive-aggressive, but it looks like they've been taking or sending people in both directions. So when you and I went to Aleronde, I think they must have come and taken us there. I want to know why and I'm not willing to leave any stone unturned. Why did they take you there when you were so sick?

I know (heard a rumor) that Teddy belonged to a club. There's no word of which one or where it met, but you can guess my suspicions. If there are other Alerondens here, I hope, with publication, they'll contact us.

While I'm on this – one more confession. I'm not sure it means what I think it does, but on one of Teddy's pages in Aleronden, he has a cryptic note in English script. It just says "As-tel." So maybe my great Aunt is one of them too, though she seems to be an irrevocably hostile one.

We know nothing of our galactic geography. Aleronde could be close, and their ships already on the way. From everything Teddy tells us, we wouldn't enjoy that.

I wonder if the apparent randomness of how and when they use the cave might be an illusion. Are Gre-tra days a different length than ours? Their calendar? Even if they can coordinate between their world and Aleronde, it would be a complex cycle from our point of view. Know any mathematicians? I think it should be possible to work it out.

Publishing isn't the issue. Sorry, but everything isn't about you.

We might be the only ones alive who appreciate the danger the human race is in, whether from the Gre-tra working to their own agenda, or from Alerondens who devour and spit out every planet they find.

I know you well enough, Curt, despite your bluster. I'm sure you realize why I didn't come clean with all this straightaway. I need you on board. We have to start recruiting. I can't do much on my own. (JW would be a good start, and I'm serious about a mathematician).

You and I must find a way to go back to Aleronde. We can't sit on this and not act.

Theo

Email CB 12Aug2011

From: Bookman@_____________.co.uk

Subject: Re: The Problem

Date: Fri, 12 Aug 2011

To: Theo05 <Theo4505@_________.tv>

You owe me a lot more than a pint.

I've thought about it. I've slept on it. I've decided.

No. I don't want to have anything to do with it.

Not for your Uncle Teddy or Aunt Marjory's memory.

Not for you, old-school ties notwithstanding.

Not for the human race or any danger you imagine for it.

And not for all the beer in Belgium.

That sound has haunted me most of my life, that singing from the warehouse.

To sit on that impossibly long marble rail on that ridiculous elevated walkway in the evening light. To hear that song again and know I'm awake?

Damn you. Maybe.

Curt

The End

Ed Charlton was born in England of a mixed marriage—his mother being English and his father a Scot. He currently lives with his wife and cat in a former colony.

Ed is happy to recommend The Write Groups of Montclair, New Jersey, and Kennett Square, Pennsylvania; IndieReader.com; an organic diet; and not letting children go unaccompanied into caves.

on can be obtained at www.ICGtesting.com

5

2B/25/P

9 781935 751243